STEPHEN L. GRESHAM

STRANGERS
TO THE
MYSTIC BEAST

THE NAHOLLO CHRONICLES
VOLUME ONE

She stumbles along like a sleepwalker, her eyes open, seeing things, I assume, that I would never wish to see. She speaks again, but her voice has changed---no longer hers---the voice of the swamp, perhaps. A voice that belongs dead.

"We're on the track that's lost its way," she says.

I feel an old belonging to those words, for I realize that what I am doing is unforgivable.

We walk on, and I am listening to the darkness, but Allegra is hearing voices beyond the human---voices she has prepared to hear---and I cannot possibly know what they are saying.

I glance now at my feet where something has slithered through the shallows. I can feel Allegra's warm breath on the back of my neck. I pull her with me back to more solid ground.

Where someone blocks our passage.

I cry out in surprise.

Night birds take wing.

As if on cue, there is lightning and thunder and a hot wind.

My lantern sprays across the small, resolute figure of Sister Speakes.

Go back," she says, tonelessly. "This is the track of dead rising. It leads to a place where no one returns alive."

I say nothing. I meet the woman's eyes, the wisdom, the knowing sunken there like buried treasure. Allegra is silent, too, yet her breathing is almost a determined growl. I can feel that despite the warning she has no choice but to continue.

Just as mysteriously as she appeared, Sister Speakes turns and walks away, swallowed at last by the wildness of the swamp.

It is time for me to do what I must do.

I tug Allegra close to me. I embrace her. Then, in a spontaneous, unexpected act, I kiss her on the cheek. I push her forward.

She goes her way.

She begins to call the Beast.

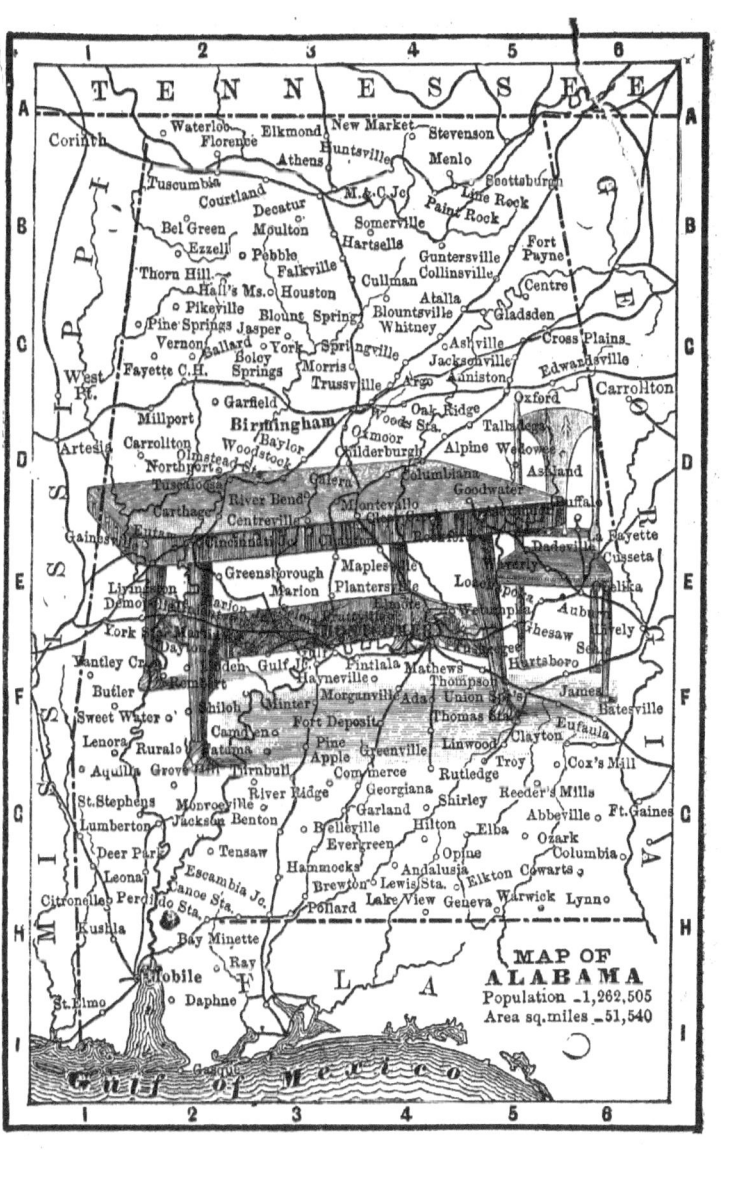

MAP OF
ALABAMA
Population _1,262,505
Area sq.miles _51,540

"Are armed, but we are strangers to the stars,
And strangers to the mystic beast and bird,
And strangers to the plant and to the mine."

—Ralph Waldo Emerson, "Blight"

ONE DAY

THE GIRL WHO WOULD NOT DIE

MET

THE MAN WHO COULD NOT LIVE

One day, the girl who would not die met the man who could not live.

I have written about that day and about some that came before and some that came after. I kept track of the days—those of the remarkable summer of 2010—and I did so at first because I wanted to; in the end, I did so because I needed to. Perhaps I had no choice. It was to be a season of unnatural and unearthly seductions.

Since I am writing these words, I obviously survived—a piece of me, that is. But I have seen things, done things, felt things: darknesses arriving and passing, poisons everywhere. Yes, I survived, and yet I am truly among the ones left behind, and I deserve to be.

Who am I?

I like to call myself, "Jessie." It is gender-deflecting shorthand for "Jessica Lovelia DeGresse." I am forty-six years old, have never been married, have never birthed a child. I am not an old maid, but rather one who has trodden the timeless paths of eros and has always lost her way. When I look in my mirror, I accept that while I am not homely, my face is unfinished. Once, a kindly, grandmotherly woman told me that I possessed a "good face." I still do not know what that expression means, but I like it.

So here I will begin.

Listen and try to understand what I have to say, but also— and much more importantly—try to understand what cannot be said. If I were able, I would offer you truths in a world of lies. Instead, I can only admit this: I made mistakes.

Horrible, unforgivable mistakes.

June 1

It is dawn on my path at the edge of the pond. Marauder, alive at first light, noses in the surrounding thicket, zigzagging, then circling in a many-angled round as if controlled by an unseen voice or an unseen hand. Jacob plods robotically along behind me; I have tempted him with an apple.

I want our father's property to be an Eden.

I suppose I know that there will be serpents of temptation.

But these scruffy, undeveloped acres are far away from the everywhere. I think they will be ideal for my purposes. Because I crave solitude, because I feel a need to be healed, I have moved in to our father's rustic cabin. Trusting that reading can help with the healing process, I have brought my books and my memories and little else. My stark, abjectly simple choice has also been motivated by a desire to watch after my Lucas, who is my one and only living sibling. He has just turned forty and, according to some, has gone strange especially since the recent passing of our father, Dalton Guy DeGresse. My mother, Tara, is alive but not with us.

I love my Lucas more than my life itself.

Light, the kind that is dew-filled and endlessly falling, toys with my path and plays across the silken stillness of the pond; a few birds flit; a few sing; and pearly bubbles—unmistakable signs of soft-shelled turtles—rise to the surface as if from a broken strand of all that is wild. The depths open at such sightings. Marauder continues to cut in and out of wild azaleas and dogwoods no longer in bloom, through sedge grass and close to pines and sweetgums, pausing occasionally to sniff deeply and issue a *pssft* at smelly molecules of interest. Jacob, his lips working around the apple like velvet, cream-colored mittens, swats at morning flies with his magnificent tail. I drink in a full measure of peace and serenity and make my way back to the cabin.

My kerosene lamp wrestles with heavy shadows. In my hearth, I set in a new fire and brew the first of my two cups of coffee. I will sprinkle both cups with raw sugar just the way our father liked it, and I will sit at my eating table—my *only* table—elbows planted firmly on its surface, and think about what I might fix my Lucas for his lunch. I will think some more about how much I love him and about how I wish he would relinquish his obsessive desire for revenge.

When the aroma of coffee fills my somber kitchen, I pour a cup and think about my reading for the day: possibly Emerson, possibly Whitman. I sigh self-pityingly, for I miss teaching. A year ago I became unemployed. Mr. Emory Forrester, headmaster of the Mahonia Christian Academy of East Alabama where I had taught English for quite a number of years, directed one morning that I come to his office where he smiled insincerely and said, "Miss DeGresse, I am truly sorry, but we are gone have to let you go." *Let me go where*? I wanted to blurt out. Of course, I knew why my services would no longer be needed. I could offer no defense or mitigating explanation for what had taken place.

Mostly, I enjoyed the young people who were my students. They did, on occasion, confuse me. They did, on occasion, frustrate or even unsettle me. But I loved teaching. More accurately, I loved the material. American Literature 111, a semester course replete with the selected works of Emerson, Thoreau, Poe, Hawthorne, Melville, Whitman, and Dickinson, was my specialty. I grew to like some of my colleagues—one much more than the others. Curious it is how the living present can be joyous and grim all at once. I am not proud of myself, yet neither will I torture myself with regret or guilt. I have always attempted to belong to myself. Does that preclude wanting to belong *with* another? I do not believe it does.

The sermon-like tone of Perry Ellis Towson calling for Jacob shakes me from my coffee reverie; I can hear his willow switch whistle-crack toward the cabin, each wicked snap of it protecting him from demons only he can sense. Barely fourteen, Perry Ellis, blind, black, and Jesus-haunted, lives with his grandmother in a derelict shanty down the road. He will be shirtless as usual, muscular, his sweat almost iridescent; he will be carrying his much-thumbed Bible in a shoulder satchel. He keeps the holy book close to him—in fact, virtually under his skin, like a tattoo. He also carries a very sharp knife attached to his belt loop: with that knife he carves marvelous objects—wooden figurines and utensils. But I suspect that it is, often as not, a weapon as well as a tool.

"Hey, mule, hey, mister! Come on ta home, Mr. Jacob! Y'all be trespassin', dude! Y'all stop on botherin' Miss DeGresse! Doncha hear me?"

I move to intercept the voice.

"Jacob likes to visit," I say, taking in Perry Ellis and his desultory approach. "He's a wonderful listener and gets along with Marauder good and fine. Might on as well let him stay."

Head down, a smile quivering at his lips, the boy on the edge of being a man parts the rays of sun along my main path. He wears the aura of a black angel, sans wings.

"Yes, ma'am, but he's got him his own home. Granny Mae, she says we need ole Jacob to be like a watch dog, doncha see?"

I chuckle at that.

"Your daddy's rusted-out, going-nowhere Chevy pickup would do as well at keeping thieves away as Jacob would."

Grinning, he stops to switch absently at the pine straw beneath his naked feet.

"I know dat's right," he says.

And so, like the good habit it is, I invite him inside and fix him coffee which he will drink only after ravaging it with enough milk and sugar to send it miles from tasting like real coffee. As is customary, I let him hold forth on his favorite subject: demons. Spittle forms on his lips, and his milky, jerky eyeballs roll pointlessly from one corner of my kitchen to the other as he narrates his latest dream—this one about demons cropping up in my woods like surprise lilies. He growls at me for laughing at the image spawned.

"Dat dream means somethin'," he claims. "Somethin' with the stain of evil comin' this way."

"Nonsense," I say.

For I am deeply agnostic, never having seen anything compelling about the anthropomorphic God—an old man, often cranky and unconvincingly loving—that the Christian mythos depicts. And God's boy, Jesus, might be pleasant enough, but I have never felt that my soul—if, indeed, I have one—has needed saving, especially by some young fellow who could use a shave and a haircut, speaks in riddles and got himself crucified. When, on occasion, I share my view with Perry Ellis, he trembles with a toothy rage and assures me that I will burn everlastingly in Hell.

We shall see.

"Y'all mean," he responds, "dat y'all don't believe God works in mysterious ways?"

"I simply mean this, Perry Ellis: I just do not know."

We have the best kind of feud.

Slurping down his coffee, he muses several moments, sculpts a stone face, and then announces that he will be taking his mule away from my godless influence. And he does. But I know, of course, that they will both return: mule *and* boy. For reasons I cannot fully comprehend, they like my company or my cabin or my property. Something draws them.

I know for a fact that Perry Ellis finds the mystery of my Lucas to be irresistible.

My guest having been claimed again by the crouched and hushed silence of my woods, the kitchen seems as quiet as a monastery. I look around at all that I do not have and shrug. I have been living in the cabin since early March, alone, but not alone enough to be holy, I suppose. The property our father deeded to my Lucas and me amounts to just under fifty acres. Most folks would say the land beneath my feet holds little worth. If I had the opportunity, I would respond to them by saying that it is worth a good deal to who I am and to who I am trying to become.

As summer arrives, I suspect that the property is haunted: by the ghost of our father and by the Beast—that is, the creature, real or imaginary, that my Lucas spends his nightly hours pursuing.

I decide I will make cornbread and fry up some potatoes and a slice of ham for his lunch. I will march it over to the mildew-covered, double-wide trailer he has parked at the far corner of our property and offer it to him. He will not, of course, say anything—perhaps nod appreciatively—and I will touch his cheek and be there for him, asking only that he hew up some firewood for me when he finds the time.

When the cornbread batter is in the oven of my ancient stove, I sit again at my table, an unopened volume of Emerson as company. I close my eyes and whisper into the indifferent silence: "What am I?"

I choose not to open my eyes to seek an answer from Emerson.

But I think maybe, just maybe, I do hear a voice from somewhere this side of madness respond.

You are the keeper of those who fall.

June 2

Astranger happened upon the cabin very early this morning.

A thick fog cradled the woods.

Marauder's barking woke me from a dream about clambering out of the depths of a cave while being exhorted, Orpheus-like, not to look back whence I had come. I did not mind being rescued from the sharp-bladed angst of that venture. At first, I thought maybe my Lucas had dispatched the Beast and, ending his wordless days, had come over to share the good news. Yet I had heard no shots.

My lamp raised to eye level, I stepped out onto the rock-and-mortar entrance area, a patio of sorts, where to my surprise Marauder was licking the fingers of a giggling girl. Bloody fingers. Rarely had I seen this Pit Bull take to an unknown scent the way he was. And never had I seen a girl such as this one: like a woodland creature exiled from a classical myth, and, having been cursed and tortured by the gods for transgressions unknown, had wandered into the pages of a new dimension where she did not belong.

"Gracious goodness," I said, when I saw that she was bleeding from her arms and legs, even from her bare feet; she looked as if she had been wrapped in barbed wire and cruelly unwound. "What in the heavens is going on here?"

She said nothing. Fed Marauder a few more licks of blood. Then staggered.

"Do not leave, young lady!"

I ran back inside for water and bandages. I also fetched two of my plastic, outdoor chairs I had bought at Wal-Mart.

A bit uncertainly, she sat down as I shooed Marauder away before he turned into a vampire. She gulped down the water like someone who had been lost for days in the Sahara. While she drank, I laid out a mound of sticks and dry sedge grass in my rock-lined, circular fire pit and struck a match to it.

In the combined light of my lantern and the start-up fire, I studied the girl even as I knelt and began to dab at her wounds: she had long, dirty-blonde hair tricked out with swatches of sticky weed; her complexion was pale and splotchy, her nose and lips tiny, almost elfin, and her eyes—her eyes were breathtakingly lovely, though the light in them began to dim as seconds passed. She wore a dingy, shapeless, colorless dress that was much too short. Her legs were deer-thin and caked with blood, but she was surprisingly large and firmly breasted. Because she was not wearing a brassiere, I could see her nipples defiantly erect. I would not allow myself to imagine whether she was wearing underpants. And something I thought initially might be a huge spider lurking menacingly on one side of her throat turned out to be the tattoo of snake fangs dripping what appeared more to be honey than venom.

Yet, the sight of it made me shudder.

She seemed oblivious to my presence as I washed at the more serious wounds and considered whether a full bandage or a series of Band-Aids would be more effective at a particular sight. I tossed softly-toned questions at her all the while, but she did not speak until I noticed that she had stopped drinking water and had started drinking in the fire.

"Flames are nice," she said in a sandpapered voice, smiling a gorgeous, albeit sad smile, her teeth as white as a full moon. It sounded as if she were speaking only to herself. Then she winced, jerking her head around anxiously as if the darkness of the after midnight, foggy woods might be in pursuit of her. "Oh, I'm fucked," she said, not changing her tone. "I lost my pack. Fucked, fucked, fucked. God damn it."

"Your pack?"

She woke, or so it seemed. She angled her head down and stared at me the way one might who has never seen another human being. When her face turned fully toward mine, I felt the velvet witchery of her eyes, and I fought the spell they unwittingly cast.

"Who the fuck are *you*?" she said.

She laughed a smoky laugh.

"Maybe your guardian angel," I said.

"No shit?"

We unfolded our introductions. I limited mine to a skeletal self. Then I smiled an invitation for her to begin. With Marauder half asleep at her feet, the girl spoke of herself as "Cavatina Carlotta McKenna," fifteen, from Sweet River, but her sudden interest in my bandaging of her wounds derailed her train of thought, and so I broke in and asked the obvious: "What are you doing out here and how did you get cut up like this?"

I must assume that she was not lying when she described a group of outsider boys and girls—her pack—that sought wooded areas to drink, do drugs, and mutilate each other. I blinked away a swarm of disbelief.

"But why on earth would you take knives to your friends and carve at their flesh?"

Her face swung up into the caress of the night. She snuffled once and shook her head.

"To feel alive. More alive. Hell, maybe to feel closer to death."

"That makes absolutely no sense, my dear."

She giggled.

"Shit, what does? I mean … fuck, you know? What the fuck *does* make sense?"

While tempted to offer some philosophical answer—perhaps from Emerson or Thoreau—I pressed, instead, to learn the whereabouts of her partners in the ritualistic bloodletting.

She glanced around as if actually looking for them.

"Who the fuck knows? Most of them are kind of assholes, you know what I mean?"

"No, I do not." I could not help staring at her, disgusted by and yet fascinated with her. "Is your language always so profane? So vile?"

She smiled confusedly and whispered, "Vile?"

"And what about your parents? Do they know that you go into the woods and allow yourself to be abused? They must be worried sick about you right this minute."

She barked out a laugh that generated several bubbles of mucous from her nose.

"Get real," she said, wiping at her upper lip with the back of her hand. "They don't give a shit. They split up years ago. My dad is off who knows where fucking anything with a cunt that'll spread her legs. My mom, she's a God damned drunk. Probably passed out in our living room with the television running."

"I am sorry to hear this," I said, and I meant it.

The marble hurt in her eyes softened as if some witchy thought chanted, drawing her to an inner moon. She smiled again, this time as if struck with a sudden recognition.

"You teach at Mahonia, right? I'm a sophomore there. You're a teacher, right?"

"I was. They had to let me go. I taught American literature." She was nodding. I quickly asked, "Do you like Mahonia?"

"God, no!" she nearly shouted. "It's a sorry-ass place. The girls are cold cunts and the boys are pricks." There was a further sizing up in her hesitation; it made me uncomfortable. This wild girl seemed to be searching for an entrance into the mystery of me. "Hey, you know what? I've heard my sister talk about you. Shit, yes. Do you remember a girl named 'Allegra McKenna?'"

In fact, I did.

A most unfortunate, terrible, tragic situation centered on her two years or so back. The girl, sixteen or seventeen at the time, had been brutally raped, strangled, and then buried, apparently still alive. But somehow she had managed to claw her way out of her untimely grave. Her attacker was never apprehended.

"The one who would not die," I said, the words sounding distant and hollow and very strange to my ears.

"Yup, my crazy-ass sister." Cavatina explained that Allegra had been recovering in a mental institution until a month ago. "She's back living at our house, you know, just trying to get her shit together."

"Is she then over her psychological problems?"

"Still seems pretty fucked up if you ask me. I mean, it's like being under the same roof with a fucking zombie, you know—a drunk *and* a zombie."

She turned away, gazing into the spectral fire as if it were a crystal ball.

I could not imagine what kind of future she saw for herself.

"Some," I said, "believe my Lucas has problems of that kind. My brother, my Lucas, well, he has been in Iraq and seen things that you cannot stop seeing and, well, love, I believe if there is enough love, a person can recover from the most unfortunate circumstances. They can recover and ..."

Of course, I instantly regretted broaching the subject of my brother's situation.

Pulling free of the flames, Cavatina spun into the trailing off of my words.

"Oh, shit, yes. Your brother. I heard about him. He's the one the war fucked over, right? Has shit for brains now, right?"

Indignant, I heaved my chest at her and exclaimed, "My Lucas will be fine. Do *not*, young lady, speak of him that way in my presence."

My heart thrummed in my earlobes.

"Hey, God damn, I'm sorry, but you brought him up." She paused. Again, something in the gesture was unsettling. "My mother, she's a failed musician—shit, she's a failed *everything*—and she, you know, when she was sober, used to talk about your brother. He was like a good singer—like really fucking good, wasn't he?"

"Yes."

"He can't sing no more?"

"Not true. He has an exceptionally wonderful voice, a heavenly voice. He can sing. He merely chooses not to." I looked away. The night held me in a grip that was not loving. "It is," I continued, "as if his voice has been locked up in a dark dungeon somewhere deep inside him." I softly patted my sternum.

I teared up.

Cavatina leaned forward.

"Shit, you gonna cry? I mean ... fuck."

"No. I am *not* going to cry. You will *never* see me cry."

I stood on shaky legs to nourish the fire.

Cavatina slid out of her chair and frisked herself.

"Oh, God damn it, I lost my cell phone." Then she focused

on her feet. "And my fucking shoes. Shit, shit, shit."

"I do not have a phone," I said, "but if you are not able to find your way home, I could have my Lucas take you in his truck."

"No phone? You shittin' me?"

I shook my head.

Scratching at her throat, she sat back down and said, "You probably don't have a cigarette I could bum, do you?"

"No, I do not."

"How about cold beer? Or some weed—you know, marijuana?"

She smiled mischievously. I told her that I did not keep beer or possess narcotics. I did not, however, volunteer that I had several bottles of scuppernong wine hidden away. I had acquired a taste for it in recent years from our father, I suppose.

As if exasperated or mystified, she tossed her delicate hands into the air.

"So what's it like living out here in the fucking wilderness?"

I told her that my life was good: that I did not feel a need for a phone, a television, a computer, a radio, or a CD player, and though my cabin lacked electricity, I had a good, deep well filled with cool, sweet water. I had a large ice box, a bucket flush toilet, and a shower of sorts. I had books. Fire took care of most of my needs otherwise.

She seemed enrapt by my narrative.

"Are you, like, in one of those fucking weird religious cults? I mean, shit, sounds like you haven't left the nineteenth century. I never met nobody who lived like this. It's like you're a fucking hermit or whatever you'd call, you know, a female hermit."

I could not repress a smile.

"I cannot say that I see myself as a hermit. I do have my Lucas and Perry Ellis and Marauder and, some days, Jacob. As far as being in a religious group—no, definitely not. That mode of thinking strikes me as hogwash."

She nodded absently as if in agreement.

"But don't you get kinda lonely?"

"'Why should I feel lonely? Is not our planet in the Milky Way?' That is a famous line from Henry David Thoreau, one of my favorite authors. Have you read him?"

She squinted her eyes. Thinking for her appeared to be the equivalent of being forced to look into direct sunlight.

"Yeah, maybe. Was he the guy that lived out by a pond and chased after a woodchuck one time so he could eat it? Kind of a fucked-up dude? Hey, you think my friends and me are crazy for cutting on each other—wasn't that dude pretty damn strange, too?"

I granted her half a point and moved on.

"It just happens that I need solitude at this stage of my life," I said. I mentioned the death of my father and that I had never been married.

She grew quiet before that impish smile of hers returned.

"Gotta ask you something: don't you miss gettin' laid?"

"Miss what?"

"You know—sex. Can't be gettin' much out here in the sticks."

I blinked away a flush of anger as I could feel myself becoming incensed and wanting to change the direction of the conversation.

"This topic is much too personal," I said, employing my classroom voice.

But Cavatina, with the ineluctable eye of a raptor, was staring at me.

"You a virgin?" She paused melodramatically. "Oh, fuck. You are, aren't you? Holy shit!"

Tiny explosions in my chest caused my voice to quaver as I lifted a forefinger and waved it into her slack, open, grinning face.

"This is enough! Enough!" I gathered a modicum of control before adding, "I do not feel a need to discuss this matter with you or anyone else. You are being impertinent, young lady."

She had me in a wounded dash for private safety, and she knew it. She smelled blood. Her smile grew bolder, more salacious—if smiles are truly capable of being salacious.

"Hey, I can do you. Really. Right now. My way of thanking you for your help. I mean, the thing is—I love sex. All kinds of sex. With guys. Girls. Men. Women. All ages. I love it." She paused to glance down at Marauder. "Not with animals, you know, dogs or nothing like that." She petted his head and whispered, "Sorry," to him. Then she met my disgusted gaze and added, "I've got good, long fingers and a kickass tongue." To punctuate her spiel, she slithered that tongue in and out, wetting her bottom lip.

For a few heartbeats, I could not seem to breathe properly.

When I was finally able to issue words, I felt that I was hearing them as in a taped delay.

"You! You are despicable. You are the most *vulgar* ..."

"And vile," she interjected. "Don't forget that one."

I stopped myself. A curious calm fell over my shoulders; I think I may even have shivered in a pleasant, self-assured way. "I am *not*," I began again, "a prude. I am, in fact, for a Southerner, a liberal-minded person. As I implied, I do not think there is a God somewhere who will strike me dead for sins written up in the Bible. But there is such a thing as decency and ... and civility and propriety. One does not need a church to embrace such concepts."

I probably said more, but I do not recall what.

"OK," she said, shrugging. "That's all cool with me. Shit, no problem."

Thereupon she got to her feet and began to dance slowly, sensually around the fire pit. As I watched her, I saw a creature whom I imagined needed sex as sustenance, whose body required it as it also required food and water. Her dance occupied a space of innocence despite what I sensed was otherwise the truth. She might, had I not stopped her, have danced herself to death.

I made her sit down because I had noticed another untreated wound. But when I returned from having gone back inside the cabin for fresh water, she was gone, leaving behind a silence that was stunning, almost mesmerizing. Even Marauder seemed tuned in to it.

Cavatina.

Had I merely dreamed this wild girl?

Had the night given birth to her?

Although she had upset me, I felt sorry for her.

I assumed that I would never see her again.

June 3

I dreamed of Cavatina's fangs.

When I was a little girl, our father warned me that when he killed a poisonous reptile such as a copperhead or rattler or cottonmouth and then beheaded it, I should be aware that the head could, on occasion, remain animated, possibly capable of inflicting harm upon anyone foolish enough to draw close to it. How good our father was at frightening me.

In my dream, the honey-venomed, snake-head tattoo rose from the skin of Cavatina's lovely throat and sought me out, becoming quite real and quite dangerous. It was Marauder who came to my rescue; he wrestled the violent head with an equally violent intensity. Then, much to my surprise if not horror, he ate the thing. Swallowed it in a crunchy, slobbery, gurgling gulp and licked his lips. Afterwards, my hero sat down with me and began to talk. Yes, Marauder talked. Once again I was surprised if not horrified.

He spoke in a hoarse, whiskey-textured voice; he told me that while he liked Cavatina, he feared my Lucas, that he thought Perry Ellis was spooky, and that he believed Jacob to be the best friend a dog could have. Naturally I waited for him to offer his views of me, but when he did, I could not, for the life of me, hear his comments. The inner screams of my anxieties drowned them out as surely as the siren of an emergency vehicle.

I woke enervated and deeply puzzled.

When I gave Marauder his breakfast bowl of dog food, I stared at him until I felt as silly as a goose. The rest of the morning I tried to read Emerson. My eyes scanned, distractedly, his fine essay, "Society and Solitude." At the conclusion of it, I murmured, "I cannot enough conceal myself."

Late morning, Perry Ellis made an appearance, not to retrieve Jacob, but rather to ask about my Lucas.

"Somethin' extra botherin' him," he said. "I knowed it."

Over coffee we chatted. I darkened with seriousness. I feared that Perry Ellis was right.

"Revenge has branded my Lucas. He has been tied to some stake within and cannot find release—the Beast baits him."

"Your daddy, he believed in dat Beast, and so do Mister Lucas. If y'all wanna know the Lord's Truth, the Beast is the Devil hisself. Dat's what I think."

"I just want my Lucas to be free—free of his obsession. When I look at him these days I see a crucifixion in his face. That is what Ishmael said of Ahab in *Moby Dick*."

Why I wasted that allusion on Perry Ellis, I do not know.

"Mister Lucas, he needs Jesus, the Son of God crucified on a tree to save every sinner from damnation."

He nodded hard to punctuate his declaration. I followed it with a comment that took me by surprise. I cannot quite understand why it came out of my mouth.

"My Lucas needs a woman," I said.

Slightly embarrassed, I glanced at Perry Ellis, his closed, scripture-hardened expression showed tiny cracks of a grin.

"Some new woman been around here? I'm thinkin' dare has."

"Yes," I said.

I gave him a brief and not-at-all flattering account of Cavatina and her visit; it was obvious that Perry Ellis, with his sensitive nose, had smelled her. Had smelled her blood and her sweat. He had, no doubt, smelled her sexuality. Most certainly, he had smelled what he would characterize as the sin that perfumed her body.

"Must be demons in her to cut herself," he said. "Demons can do dat. They can make a someone harm the temple dat's your body."

"Demons. Your answer for everything, is it not?"

"Yes, Miss DeGresse. Pretty much so."

"You know, Perry Ellis, I would not mind if one day you

called me 'Miss Jessica.' We are, after all, becoming friends despite there being worlds between us spiritually."

"Yes, Miss DeGresse."

And so I sent Perry Ellis on his way and fixed two lettuce and tomato sandwiches and pork rinds for my Lucas. The tomatoes were store bought; later this summer I hope to have some homegrown ones. On the concrete block steps leading to the door of his trailer, I saw hunting boots. They belonged to my Lucas. They were slightly muddy, but I did not mind. I put down the plate of sandwiches and I hugged those boots to my bosom and imagined my Lucas inside sleeping or perhaps just rousing awake.

I wanted to be in bed with him, holding him, loving him.

I wanted him to end his mad, nightly tracking of the Beast.

I blamed our father. The Beast is his creation.

He claimed that he was attacked on two occasions by something in these woods. The first time was a couple of summers ago near dawn when, on one of his rambles, a large creature slammed into him from behind, then tore away before he could see what it was. Not injured seriously—a bruised thigh and a twisted knee—he, regardless, was left quite shaken by the episode. Most unsettling to him was the fact that he could not determine whether whatever lay waste to him had been a four-legged or a two-legged creature. Then again last September another attack, this one more serious. This one at twilight: the Beast—as he called it—charged him front on; apparently the sight of it so terrified our father that his heart momentarily failed him, all bodily functions shut down, he passed out, and for several hours he lay unconscious. He suffered what amounted to a minor stroke, and his respiratory system incurred lasting damage.

Later, he could not even provide us with a description of the Beast. Yet, he suggested that it might not be of this world. For my part, I began to imagine a blob of dark energy slouching through the woods, a phantom of everything men have ever feared. But, in truth, I did not and still do not believe there is a Beast.

Our father, no doubt, encountered *something*—perhaps a

large, stray dog—just not a supernatural entity.

Why he chose to build his so-called Beast into a mythic monster is beyond me.

He succeeded, however, in convincing my Lucas that a hideous thing stalked our property, possibly having a lair in the Nahollo Swamp or in the Cat Bells cave system, both of which are adjacent to our land.

At the door to his trailer, my Lucas opened to my knocking; his blond-haired, blue-eyed handsomeness seemed drained like our pond drying up, receding to soupy algae during a drought.

"What is wrong, sweetheart?" I said.

His hair was long now, reaching his shoulders, much in contrast to the military style crew cut he used to wear. Not meeting my eyes, he took the plate, gestured for me to leave, and disappeared into his shadows.

I was heartsick.

During the long, late afternoon hours, I took my sorrow and dread with me on my most distant path, the one that winds by the nearly hidden, back entrance to Cat Bells and merges with a dirt-bike trail bordering the vast Nahollo Swamp before falling away to the steep banks of Deep Kill Creek. Marauder and Jacob accompanied me. Did they sense how blue I was?

I watched for snakes. I almost wished to be bitten by one.

Passing showers and oppressive humidity forced me back to the cabin.

To get my Lucas off my mind, I made myself think of my favorite writers and their marvelous works: incoherent snatches of Whitman's "The Mystic Trumpeter" swam through my thoughts. Out of nowhere, I recalled that our father played the trumpet when he was a young man in New Orleans.

I thought of Cavatina. I did not want to. I thought of her and her unfortunate sister, Allegra. I heard echoes of Cavatina's filthy language—it hurt my ears. It angered me. And I found myself comforted by recalling that such profanity does not appear on the pages of an Emerson or a Hawthorne or even a Poe. Would, I asked myself, my dear Emily Dickinson employ trashy language in her fabulous poems? Would she, I asked myself, have been tempted to revise that gem of a poem beginning, "I am

alive—I guess—" to read:
  "How fucking good—to be alive!
  How fucking infinite, God damn it—to be
  Alive—"?
  Well, perish the thought. Cavatina had made me feel puri-
tanical—old and cold. Perhaps she had stirred a yellow jacket's
nest of nerves. Yes, perhaps so. Should I admit that I am unlov-
able? Who, I asked myself, could ever want me for warmth of
the flesh?
  By the time the afternoon had faded, I convinced myself
that I hated Cavatina. *Cavatina*—what kind of name is that, any-
way? I hoped she never showed her face on my property again.

June 4

There are moments in life in which Madness tells her own story.

I wake with that thought; I rustle through a box of old photographs in my bedroom until I find the one I am after: Tara Amelia DeGresse, my mother. No, she was *not* named for the plantation in *Gone with the Wind*; the name had existed in her family, the Burnside clan, for several hundred years as her people moved from Scotland to Ireland and, eventually, to Virginia and on to Alabama.

The black-and-white photo is badly creased in one corner; likewise, my mother looks badly creased: she is thin, her eyes sunken, her dress almost a shroud—she could nearly pass for a Holocaust survivor. I do not know who snapped this particular photo, but I do know that it was taken not long after the death of my infant sister, Alice. My mother is seated in a rocking chair on our porch in Sweet River; she is not engaging the lens of the camera, her eyes being drawn to whatever strange worlds grief has opened for her. Ever so delicately, she is cupping her chin with long, narrow fingers—I sense that the hand is trembling. I sense something more: she is slipping into dementia. She is becoming Madness herself, sanity being siphoned off even as the timeless, antic disposition moments pass. Over my coffee I stare at the photo until looking is not enough, and yet looking is all that is possible.

Around lunch, my Lucas shows up to cut wood. He enters the cabin tentatively, rather like a yard dog that knows he should not be inside. I almost weep at the sight of him. He is wearing overalls with no shirt underneath; his eyes are radiantly mournful. I pull his head to my bosom, but he stiffens. Then he straightens and nods and exits to complete his appointed task. Marauder cowers from him, and Jacob seems, as well, to keep his distance. I stand on the back porch and watch my Lucas wield the heavy axe. He is, I assume, thinking of the Beast.

But I am not.

A rainy morning in early March not long after I had moved in to the cabin catches in my web of memory. It was the morning my Lucas came to me with a request that I wish I had been courageous enough to deny. There was, I recall, a desperate cast to his eyes as he set in an armload of firewood. We took chairs at the eating table, but he was not hungry, not for food.

"Can you get in touch with Daddy?"

I wagged my head to deflect his question.

"Our father has passed away. He has not been with us since January."

My Lucas gritted his teeth.

"You know what I mean."

I did, of course.

"No," I said, quite calmly, yet firmly. "I cannot. I shall not."

But then the tone of hopelessness in his voice shattered me.

"Please," he begged. "You've helped so much before. One more time. Please."

The history he alluded to went back to when I was fourteen or so and he was eight or nine, a period in which I would often boldly claim that I was a "seer" with powers to communicate with the deceased, both the famous and the not famous. My boast was all in fun. Not, however, to my Lucas. But to please him—and I so wanted to please him, even then—I would have him sit across the table from me and we would hold outstretched hands and close our eyes in the near darkness, and I would launch into my charade. Presidents frequently spoke to me from the shadows; of course, then, I would relay their messages to my Lucas: George Washington, Abe Lincoln, and John F. Kennedy were among those who offered wisdom to him—"Do well in school. Do not be mean to animals."—that kind of thing.

And yet, years later, when my Lucas returned from his

second tour of duty in Iraq, having been given a medical discharge, the spook game grew more serious. My Lucas asked me to contact a few of his buddies who had been killed in combat or on patrol. I did not want to comply. I felt foolish. My deception seemed cruel. Unconscionable. But I loved my Lucas; I would have done anything for him. Anything. His pleading squeezed the blood from my heart. And so I would negotiate a minefield in which I had to fake the identities of young men who had known my Lucas. I managed to get good at it: "Do you remember," I would say, "that song we used to sing in our barracks? Do you remember the girl I was crazy about?"

It worked. Moreover, it seemed to bring pleasure and even a closure of sorts to my Lucas. When we finished a session, he would thank me; often he would kiss me, either on the cheek or the forehead, and that kiss would coil warmth down through my chest and between my legs and give my feet a toasty feel. I could not resist his requests.

The rain pattered softly on the roof of the cabin that morning in March. We held hands across the table; we closed our eyes. When the beating of my treacherous heart slowed, I spoke into the gloom, seeking out the spirit of our father. I tried to turn the screw of deception one more turn: "Our father is not responding. I do not believe he wants to speak to us."

Something, in the meanwhile, had besieged my Lucas.

He trembled; his eyes flew open; he yanked his hands from mine and stood up, staring beyond me, terrified, and then, seemingly, enrapt. Listening. Listening. Listening ever so intensely. I could not manage to pull him from the trance or whatever was afflicting him.

Minutes later, exhausted, his expression a mask of resolve, he sat down across from me and said, "Daddy told me what I must do, and I must do it. He said I must get revenge. He said I must not rest easy until the Beast is destroyed."

I protested. I even tossed out a feeble explanation of how I had duped him over the years regarding communications with the dead, but my Lucas would have none of it.

He thanked me lovingly. Oblivious to the rain, he left the cabin. He has not spoken a word since that morning. And I have been left with the shadow of a brother, a character from an end-less fiction, a combination of Hamlet and Ahab, with a narrative inevitability that makes me shudder.

I am culpable.

It has been useless to try to dissuade my Lucas from his maniacal mission.

Like Hamlet and Ahab, he has become a man filled with riddles.

On that day, revenge usurped the spirit of my Lucas.

On that day, my Lucas became a man who could not live.

I let go of that day and concentrate upon the moment: I fix my Lucas a bacon and egg omelet. After he has replenished my wood supply, he wolfs down the food and returns, I assume, to his trailer, and tonight he will set sail again upon the seas of revenge.

The Beast is his murderous, usurping uncle; the Beast is his white whale.

I think about the wretched condition of his trailer, for in the last several months, my Lucas has become a hoarder, his rooms a spreading cancer of chaos: clothes everywhere, plastic bags of rocks and dirt and dead vegetation, and, most unnervingly, coils of wiring for explosives, stacks of pistol and rifle shells, guns—a veritable arsenal of them—and a metal cabinet upon which he has drawn, in black marker, a skull and crossbones. I believe the cabinet houses poisons or diabolical chemicals of some sort.

His living area is a nightmare.

He no longer allows me to enter it. I do not, in truth, wish to, except to hold him.

What I truly wish is to rescue him.

My Lucas.

Lost brother.

Perhaps in this case Perry Ellis is right when he maintains that my Lucas is possessed by demons; they inhabit him like the wind or like summer humidity.

At twilight, I take a walk. Marauder scares up a feral pig. The property is getting thick with them as they broaden their range, moving out with impunity from Nahollo Swamp. Jacob nags at me for an apple. I follow my path up to the small, dark entrance to Cat Bells and try to imagine what it would be like to traverse the labyrinthine cave system. I want to enter it, but I lack the courage—and that, I believe, is the point: it takes courage to live in the world. I do not apologize for the cliché.

Night falls.

I sit near the flames of my fire pit and read Thoreau, the chapter in *Walden* entitled, "Solitude," and I long for his ability or capacity to be alone. I close my eyes and imagine Solitude as a Frankenstein creature, hulking and speechless, more like Boris Karloff in that old movie than the actual monster, so articulate and humane, in Mary Shelley's novel. Solitude looks at me with his ugly face; he is sad, rejected, orphaned. I try not to think of my Lucas. I read Emerson, his essay on Thoreau. I am cheered when I read that Thoreau, according to Emerson, "could find his path in the woods at night."

Should one envy a man's intimacy with his paths?

I think not.

In my bedroom, I light a half-dozen candles. I love candlelight. Always have. I undress. Naked, I stand before my full-length mirror bathed in the nimbus of small, flickering flames, and I study the stranger before me. I feel myself merging with that unknown, haunting figure. The deflated bulbs of my breasts seem to melt and drip down my body. I rake my fingers through my cascading, black hair, streaked as it is these days with grayish-white strands.

I touch my tongue to my lower lip.

I long to be a sorceress.

I long to enchant.

June 5

"Read your fate, see what is before you, and walk on into futurity."

Thoreau's voice compels. "Sounds"—that arresting chapter from *Walden*—lives in my morning solitude and silence. I, too, joining Thoreau, want to grow "like corn in the night"—I want to be indifferent to the superficial irritations of my emotions. I want to be a strong, whole woman. But the sour truth is that when I lapse into one of my dark, uncertain moods, I am half witch and half fate.

Thoreau reminds me to listen to Nature.

This morning I truly am. I share his love of the wailing, doleful responses of owls, the melancholy foreboding in their hoots; owls seem to remind me that Nature has given me one life and that I should not wish for an afterlife. When one prays or petitions, she is talking to herself. I am at peace with that. I am not, however, at peace with eros.

My volume of Thoreau in my lap, I sit in front of my cabin and hear, coming from the woods, a language I shall not ever learn to speak. Marauder and Jacob are off somewhere greeting the day, at one with themselves because they do not have a divided consciousness. My Lucas is probably asleep; the Beast is wherever monsters need to be. I am thinking of love lost.

His name was Landon Breyer; he was my colleague at Mahonia Christian Academy. He taught science. His lab classroom exuded the rotten egg odor of sulphur with an overlay of formaldehyde. Though he tried to get me to do so, I was never able to look directly at a dissected frog. Now I finally understand that love can be so brutal that it dissects us—whether anyone else is aware or not.

He—this Mr. Breyer—befriended me. Married to an invalid woman, he had no children nor any desire to have any. He was, nonetheless, popular with students who adored his puckishness, his gregarious manner, and what they perceived to be his generous spirit. While not a handsome man, he possessed a lovely, infectious smile which, when he flashed it, caused me to forget that he was somewhat short with a rather protruding stomach and a rapidly balding head. He was light on his feet, a pinball machine of frenetic activity, and his ability to know just what to say to expunge my gloom bordered on being psychic.

He won my heart.

I thought I had won his.

There were good times. Many, in fact. But my memory cannot rise to embrace them. Instead, I hear his softly spoken, yet devastatingly final words: "I can't make this happen, Jessie. I'm sorry. Very sorry."

I shrieked back at him like a wronged female from a Greek drama. I was Medea. I was Antigone.

"You, sir, are a coward! You are weak and treacherous!"

I wanted to throw beakers and test tubes and flasks at him.

I wanted to poison him.

In a way, I poisoned myself.

There was more to the story. Much more. An aftermath. However, I am not yet prepared to re-visit those moments on these pages. I live in the churning flow of "now what?"

Shedding my old life, leaf by leaf?

Reading my fate? Walking on into futurity?

Glad am I that Thoreau is not here in the flesh to chastise me.

Confession: I have been deceiving myself in still another way. I vaguely assumed that I had been writing in this journal for my eyes and ears only, but as I re-read my entries I hear, quite obviously, in the tone and mode of them, that I am sharing my words with at least one other. Long ago, a writer would allude to such a person as "Gentle Reader." I like that. But then again, if I am leading someone by the hand through my life, through these summer days, I would like to be introduced to my companion.

Whose hand am I holding?

June 6

Ijust want to be wanted.

   Perhaps only another woman can understand what I mean.

June 7

I woke this morning and thought to myself: *this is where I belong.* First light spills along the path that takes me close to the trailer where my Lucas should be returning any moment from his nocturnal trek. I am spying. I feel a delicious guilt that begins to taste bad after ten minutes or so. Am I a stalker? Just when I assume that I have missed his return, there he is, the buckle on the shoulder strap of that sleek, yet ugly, high-powered rifle with its obscene scope glinting as if tricked out with dew. My Lucas does not see me.

He is more than alone.

At the door to his trailer, he stops, and I must duck out of sight, for he glances around as if sensing that he is being watched. I wonder whether he thinks the Beast has been tracking him instead of the other way around. He coughs away the last remnant of night air and slips inside. I have to battle against a tremendous urge to follow him within.

My Lucas. So many selves. An alive self. A dead self. A dying self, but not a *living* self. Now he is a song-less self; he needs to be, once again, a singing self. Now he is a self with revenge beating where his heart once beat, with poison flowing where blood once flowed.

He loves *only* our father because our father poisoned his capacity to love anything or anyone else. When the Beast wounded our father, it inflicted the same wounds *inside* my Lucas, far beneath the skin. In the scheme of literary allusions, he became as cunningly half-brained as Hamlet, as bitterly one-legged as Ahab.

Back at the cabin, I feed Marauder and Jacob. It appears that

Perry Ellis has given up his daily task of retrieving his mule, so now he has left a large bag of feed, a mixture of oats and some other grain. With the animals contented, I fix myself a bowl of grits. I salt and butter them. I like them thick, not runny, edible with a fork. Our father did not like runny grits either. One morning many years ago, I served him up a bowl of unsatisfactory grits; he swore at me and threw the offering in my face. My Lucas, on the other hand, will eat anything, but now he takes only one meal per day. I worry over how thin he is getting.

I glance at Emerson's *Nature* as I enjoy my grits. I murmur in response to some of his more ridiculous words, "Is he serious?" And I try to think of myself as a transparent eyeball. I chuckle. Yet, in Emerson's defense, I suppose he has created a working metaphor. As I read further, I hear the echo of a loud voice. Marauder barks twice, then swallows a wet growl when I tell him to hush. The voice is coming from the pond: Perry Ellis is there practicing his preaching style, cranking up the volume enough that I will be drawn to hear him—it is a game he plays. So I finish my grits, put away Emerson, and go to listen and marvel at the boy's histrionics.

I station myself across the pond from him. He is in his usual spot, just in front of a granite boulder that is as large as a pickup truck; he has on his Sunday shirt—white, long-sleeved—and suspenders, his only pair of dress slacks and his uncomfortable, reddish-brown, wing-tip shoes. He has the Bible in his right hand, holding it open as if it is a gutted fish; he pretends to be reading it. If he is quoting scripture, I have no idea which book is his source. It does not matter, for Perry Ellis has been seduced by all the darkness Christianity harbors—damnation, a plethora of sins, most but not all of them deadly, and, of course, demons. I listen for the better part of fifteen minutes. He lathers up to a close. He knows I am watching, and so he shuts his eyes, raises his arms, and prays, the prayer managing to include me, my Lucas, his Granny Mae, his deceased mother and his derelict father, a litany of adult brothers and sisters, and a legion of cousins, aunts, and uncles.

Not sarcastically, I shout "Amen!" and invite him to come by the cabin tonight. "I shall read stories or poems. You are welcome to have a glass of scuppernong wine and enjoy your-self. My Lucas might be there."

"Dare be demons in wine," he calls out in response.

"Not mean ones," I tease.

Surprisingly, both Perry Ellis and my Lucas do, on occasion, attend in what has become a pleasant ritual of sorts, one I started in early May when evenings first invited one to linger around the fire pit and tell stories to the dark. I make a note to myself that I shall read Poe.

Twilight finds a path to my cabin.

It will be a clear, warm, starry evening.

Because it always comforts Perry Ellis, I haul out my bot-tle tree and hang my lantern from one of its limbs. I do not, of course, embrace the belief here in the South that colorful, empty bottles strung together will frighten away evil spirits. But when Perry Ellis hears the wind tinkle, tinkle the bottles, he eases into the moment and smiles more.

I stoke my fire pit. I have chairs and camp stools as if I am holding a revival. I have retrieved two bottles of scupper-nong wine and a few small glasses that once held dried beef. The wine comes courtesy of Mr. Tobias Bonnard, a neighbor who operates a tavern at the edge of Nahollo Swamp. Known as "T-Bone," Mr. Bonnard is a giant of a man who would not, unless provoked, harm anyone on this earth. Once upon a time, he was the county sheriff; he was a friend of our father, and has always been kind to me and my Lucas. I believe he was once sweet on my mother.

I have a volume of Poe. Marauder and Jacob are nearby, positioned almost as if they are extras in a nativity scene. I sigh. I feel that I have reached a state of both outer and inner readi-ness. I am waiting, prepared for whatever annunciations may transpire.

"Y'all ta home, Miss DeGresse?"

Perry Ellis emerges from the gloaming. He is carrying a large corn knife or machete. I toss a joke at him about demons, and he volleys, "I got to protect my soul, Miss DeGresse."

"Does not your Jesus do that for you?"

"The Lord promises His followers eternal life—here on dis

earth, a body got to take care of hisself." He swings the weapon forcefully.

He has no sooner sat down than my Lucas arrives, shuffling in with shadows looming at his slumped shoulders; he has that terrible rifle and a long flashlight. He seems darkly preoccupied.

I welcome them. I offer wine. My Lucas takes a glass, and, to my surprise, so does Perry Ellis.

"You must promise," I say to him, "not to turn me in for providing alcohol to a minor."

"No'am, I won't. The Lord, He tell us believers sometimes dis be no sin."

But he sits nervously, one leg jerking as if he is about to take flight.

"I thought you all would enjoy Poe this evening."

Both of them seem indifferent to my comment. After a sip of wine to wet my reading voice, I forge on, leafing through pages to find my place. However, Marauder begins to bark, and my Lucas stands, rifle readied for the approach of some thing or someone.

Could it be the Beast?

No, much to my surprise, it is Cavatina.

I hear her speak as she approaches.

"Hey, it's me. Remember?" When she enters among us, she follows with, "I like it here. Oh, shit—you havin' a party? You good with me crashin' in on it?"

"Goodness," I say, "it is not a party. Not really. On occasion, I read to my young men."

"Cool. That's just bitchin' cool. Oh, you gotta fuckin' bottle tree—so cool."

I introduce her to Perry Ellis and my Lucas; they seem a bit puzzled and skeptical of her. On her side, Cavatina is all smiles and giggles. I offer her a glass of wine, thus deepening my criminal offense, I suppose, and yet I do not feel that I am truly corrupting anyone. Life, I conclude on the spot, long ago corrupted Cavatina.

I am pleased to see that she has cleaned up; her hair has been washed and combed, the firelight catching it gently and fetchingly. She has on a touch of makeup, and I notice that she has a cluster of shiny, stud earrings and one stud piercing her skin just beneath her lower lip. The snake fang tattoo seems to hiss alluringly, but I am quite certain I am only imagining it. She wears a black tank top cut low enough that cleavage shows— at least this evening she has on a brassiere. Her blue jeans are tight; her ankle-high boots have spiky heels. She is, in fact, an attractive girl despite obvious signs on her bare arms that her cuttings have not completely healed.

"Hey," she announces as we settle back, "you guys wanna burn doobie? That's what they said back in the fucking Eighties." And she laughs a husky laugh.

I have no idea what she is alluding to. My Lucas nods. Perry Ellis murmurs, "No, thanks." He is sniffing the air; I believe that Cavatina has stirred him.

From a shoulder purse rather similar to the one Perry Ellis carries, she takes two crudely wrapped cigarettes and a lighter.

"Is that marijuana?" I say.

"Sure as shit. You want some?"

I shake my head. I am suddenly haunted by a vision of being arrested. I try to relax. And soon a sweet, sultry aroma permeates our gathering as Cavatina and my Lucas light up and smoke curls lazily, almost mystically, from them. Perry Ellis sniffs. He frowns. Takes a sip of wine and smacks his lips. The frown disappears.

For a moment, the gods of silence bless us.

The oncoming of night is good.

I glance around. Lantern light and fire pit flames coalesce, painting the countenances of my companions; I feel buoyed by the ineffable and a second drink of wine, and I say, "You all have good faces. I toast to you. To us."

I raise my glass, and so do they, Perry Ellis being a second or two tardy. We take a drink for closure. Cavatina giggles. My Lucas stares off into the woods. Perry Ellis surrenders to the flicker of a smile at the corners of his mouth. He likes, I believe, the scent of Cavatina. Then, after another sip of wine, he says, "The Lord He blesses shadows, too."

Cavatina blows smoke and rocks back as she empties her first glass of wine.

"This is so fucking cool," she exclaims.

For some reason, I do not mind her language so much tonight.

I open a second bottle of wine. My Lucas feeds the fire pit.

I clear my throat and adjust my reading glasses.

"I wish to read to you Poe's immortal classic, 'The Fall of the House of Usher.' It is a deliciously eerie tale."

I wade into the story, and I am pleased with the sound of my voice. I lead my listeners into a haunted world from which our narrator will barely escape. I am thrilled that my motley audience appears glued to every word. The story seems shorter than I have ever found it to be. I pitch the ending melodramatically, and when I look up from the final line, Perry Ellis has an opaque yet thoughtful cast to his expression; my Lucas is staring at the fire, mesmerized, as if he were seeing the dark tarn in front of the Usher house. Cavatina has her mouth open; she might be falling asleep, or that is what I assume until she blinks rapidly.

"Holy shit! That was a damn good story. And, I mean, it's like … you really can read it the right way. Fuck, that was good."

"Thank you," I say. "Perry Ellis, what did you think of it?"

His eyes narrow. He frowns. Works his mouth comically.

"It was scary. Very scary, y'all know. Dat man, he try to bury his sister. But I don't know why."

He shakes his head. I glance at my Lucas. He smiles shyly. I want to believe that he enjoyed my reading, for, years ago, he loved to have me read to him.

"I've got an idea about the story." Cavatina is looking directly at Perry Ellis as she speaks. "You think maybe they were havin' sex? Brother and sister. You know … what's that called? Incest?" She glances at me, her brow wrinkled.

I protest the interpretation, mentioning as an alternative reading that some believe Madeline to be a vampire.

"No, shit?"

Cavatina seems quite taken with the notion, but she presses for a response from Perry Ellis. He rolls his head from shoulder to shoulder.

"I don't know. I jus' don't know. Seem like the whole house, it filled to the rafters with demons."

Cavatina cackles. My Lucas laughs a soft laugh.

I wade in: "Our Perry Ellis finds demons everywhere."

I think about possibly reading another tale or perhaps a poem or two, but at that moment we hear a crashing off in the distance as if something rather large is on the run. My Lucas grabs his rifle and charges off, without hesitation, in that direction. Perry Ellis, corn knife in hand, heads off as well, leaving Cavatina and me behind.

"What the fuck?" she says.

I give her an abbreviated account of the Beast. She is in wide-eyed wonderment, though perhaps the wine and the marijuana are to blame. We sit and chat a bit longer. Soon, however, Cavatina fades.

"Shit," she says, "you mind if I flop down here tonight? I'm feelin' kind of wasted."

Part of me, of course, objects. Another part, a stranger to me, says, "No, that would be fine."

I unfold a cot that our father used to sleep on when he would steal away from town and stay in the cabin all night. I set it up in the kitchen. After Cavatina has used my bathroom, she curls up on the cot, and I throw a blanket over her. I say good night, and I am about to leave when she reaches up and hugs my neck.

"Thanks," she whispers. "I think you're a pretty fucking cool lady. Not like a bitchy teacher."

My face burns a surprised blush.

"I shall take that as a compliment. Sleep well."

I start to ask whether we should let someone know that she will not be coming home, but I reason not to. Does anyone out there care where she is? I doubt it.

Cavatina turns once and props her head in her palm.

"Hey, I like your brother—shit, I mean, he's hot. Real, real quiet and sexy. He got a girlfriend?"

"No," I say. Then, pointlessly, I add, "He barely has a life."

She nods. Blinks. Snuffles.

"I like the nigger boy, too. Is he, like, all the way blind?"

I dig my hands into my hips. My jaw tightens.

"I do not approve of that term. It is a crude, dehumanizing word. Perry Ellis is a fine young man in many respects. As

I understand, he has been sight impaired since birth. I do not believe he is able to see much if anything."

"Oh, shit, I'm sorry I called him a 'nigger boy.' I meant it in a good way. Fuck, I won't say it again."

"Thank you," I whisper, and I wonder why she exasperates me so much.

I resist a sudden urge to give her a motherly kiss. I think she needs one.

She is a child of never.

I lie awake searching for myself in the silent aftermath of the evening. I am astonished at how tightly I cling to my inner life. I do so because much that happens in my outer life is totally mystifying to me.

June 8

Sometimes there are two paths and neither takes me.

So I stand where the thicket growth has devoured a narrowing of my walking space. My head buzzes dully from last night's wine. Am I thinking clearly? I believe that I am. The paths I allude to are internal paths: one snakes along in a dark forest of self-realization, its destination—solitude. There I shall be able to fall deeply into who I must become. This path leads to a *temenos,* a sacred spot, a safe spot where healing will take place, where I will kneel at the altar of my essential self and worship the mystery of me.

But this morning another path calls; I want to refuse the call, but I am not certain that I can. Would it not be easier if we did not have to choose? Should not a path abduct us? I think it should. I long for it to. This second path leads away from solitude, meandering through clarification and anxieties until it reaches the heart of community. This path ends in the midst of people, like my young associates. Are there others whose faces I cannot yet see?

I did not move in to our father's cabin for this.

When I reach out and press my hand against the rough bark of a giant, water oak, I cannot keep from thinking of my Lucas, Perry Ellis, and Cavatina—the latter has, in fact, taken up residence in my thoughts. I did not invite her, did I?

Waking this morning, I almost jumped out of bed, for I found myself wanting to fix that young lady a good breakfast, something to offset a few of her non-salubrious habits. I envisioned eggs, grits, biscuits, and milk. I would serve her up breakfast just the way ... well, just the way a loving mother

would, a thing missing in her life. I even half-desired to watch
her eat and hear her babble, "Oh, this is so fucking good!"

Reducing profanity might follow a nice breakfast. Or so I
projected.

I even hummed as I dressed. When was the last time I
hummed as I dressed?

But she had gone.

Her cot was more than empty. An almost palpable wave
of disappointment washed over me. I hunkered down by the
cot, took the blanket in my hands and raised it to my nose—
Cavatina, the fragrance of youth battered and bold, clambering
along a thorny path through moment-to-moment futurity.

I got to my feet and felt foolish.

I am *not* her mother.

I am no one's mother and never will be.

That path did not take me.

My odd bout with disappointment sent me on this walk.
Knowing I am not capable of resolving the dilemma of the two
paths, however, I return to my kitchen, brew a cup of coffee
and think of Whitman, and of how I long to be a female ver-
sion of him—a Good Path human being. I long for him to be
waiting at the end of one of my literal paths, and I think of two
lines of his from "Song of Myself":

This hour I tell things in confidence,
I might not tell everybody but I will tell you.

For me, that "you" is my reader, whoever you are.

Do *not* let go of my hand. Please.

I am sipping a second cup of coffee when Perry Ellis sham-
bles in. Has he not gotten any sleep? He looks like a punctured
tire. He says nothing until I pour his coffee, disguised as such
with sugar and cream, and he scalds his tongue.

"Mister Lucas, he crazy."

"How so?"

I listen to a disjointed account of my Lucas and last night's
relentless chase after the Beast, of a tracking into the swamp
as if pursuing a grim, phantom future. My Lucas, according
to Perry Ellis, has supernatural stamina. But the Beast eluded
him. Or did he elude the Beast? Perry Ellis was left behind to

wonder about how things truly exist.

I do not like to discuss the Beast, so I change the subject.

"Perry Ellis, what can you see?" I say. "Do you have *any* sight?"

He frowns, layers of frowns, in fact, and works his mouth as if his jaw has come unhinged. I stifle a laugh. Eventually he glances in my direction and says,

"I might could see rainbows in da night."

I am somewhat stunned.

"Why, that is rather poetic, my friend."

But neither his blindness nor poetry is what is of interest to him. I can tell that he is incubating a question even as he slurps noisily at his coffee.

"Dat girl dat smokes pot—she very pretty?"

I study him, the features of his face coalescing.

"Yes. Yes, if you mean 'Cavatina,' yes, I would judge that she is pretty." I pause. "Do you like her?"

His expression collapses into a tangle of anxieties.

"She be in my head."

"Like a demon?"

When he turns my way again, it is difficult for me not to believe that he sees me as clearly as day.

"I gotta go pray for an answer."

"Perry Ellis, it is only natural—only human—for people, at times, to be attracted to each other. Especially young people."

"Maybe it might could be so."

He leaves, carrying his consternation over his shoulder like a heavy bag.

Later, when I take a tuna sandwich and some cold pork and beans to my Lucas, I say, "Did you like Cavatina?"

He seems edgy, preternaturally alert. He shrugs nervously. We sit on his concrete block steps, and he eats his food quickly.

I press. "Do you think she is attractive?"

He hesitates. Nods. Swallows. He does not give away much.

I take his empty plate and fork.

"I believe that Perry Ellis is smitten with her. She has a sister who is not well."

He looks away, seemingly indifferent, his attention drawn to the woods, or perhaps it is to his inner world, to the wilderness of his thoughts where the ghost of our father stalks him, making him prey to the call of revenge.

I glance up into the sunny, high sky and imagine that it is night.

And that the love I have for my Lucas is the color of a rainbow.

June 9

L ittle rivers of bird song flow through the dawn.
I am waiting for my Lucas to drive me to Sweet River's
Wal-Mart to do my grocery shopping. I hope that he has remembered; I hope that he is not too exhausted from his hunt for the
Beast.

When I woke earlier, I thought that I had heard a prowler.
Inside my cabin, hanging just above the front door, is a double-bladed hatchet I keep in case I feel threatened and cannot flee in
time to seek the help of my Lucas.

But there was, to my relief, no intruder.

Instead, the ghost of our father lurks.

At least, I believe that is what I am imagining. I have both
heard and sensed his presence before this. He skulks around
behind the cabin; so far, he has not chosen to come inside.

I know why he has returned.

I think I know why he is so angry.

What I imagine—what I can *almost* see—is a filmy outline of
him looking rather like paintings I have seen of the abolitionist, John Brown: the Old Testament beard, the eyes of a venomous serpent, and the face lit from a fire within that cannot be
extinguished.

The ghost of our father is a skilled haunter.

I believe he comes around to tear holes in my sanity.

On the way to Sweet River, I talk about Hawthorne. I cannot
be certain that my Lucas hears or comprehends what I am saying. I like Hawthorne. I like it that he understands witchy ways.
I like it that he seems to inhabit an inner realm in which *sin* is
something that one commits mostly against one's self.

My Lucas looks haunted, yet beautiful, and I love him.

I revel in being seated beside him in the cab of his truck—just the two of us—on the county road. I pretend that we are running away together, perhaps to the *ultima thule*, wherever that may be. The reality is that my Lucas will sit in his truck in the largely empty parking lot of Wal-Mart while I go in with my grocery list. Shopping very early lessens the possibility that I will see someone I know. I wear a plain dress, sensible shoes, and no makeup.

As we pull back into our property, we stop at our rural box; it is rusting and in need of paint. Once again, it is filled with junk mail: offers for cable TV service, political flyers, and notices from banks touting their latest credit cards. I will burn it all in my fire pit.

I have, in addition to the junk mail, received a letter.

It is postmarked Birmingham. It is from my Aunt Julia.

I am certain that it contains news of mother. I say as much to my Lucas. He does not seem to care.

My stomach roils as I heft the letter and anticipate its narrative.

I shall wait until tomorrow to open it.

Likely, it contains memories of the future.

June 10

My batch of cornbread this morning would not even taste good to the dead.

My heart is not in preparing food; I am stalling. Anxiety paralyzes me.

The temperature will reach the nineties by afternoon.

The letter—I imagine it to be a small, yet poisonous reptile coiled, ready to strike if I reach for it—rests on the table where I left it. My coffee cup chitters on the saucer as I steel myself. The envelope weighs darkly. Nothing good is in the air.

You need to know something about my Aunt Julia Burnside, mother's older sister, a woman who despises men and has always been very protective of her little sister, her only sibling. For her steadfast love of mother, I am grateful. When my infant sister died and mother turned strange and our father cast a cold eye upon his wife of many years, Aunt Julia rescued the woman. When it appeared mother might well be institutionalized, she stepped in. Took her away. To Birmingham. There mother has been living for what seems an eternity.

On a day after our father passed in January, my Lucas drove me to Birmingham. Mother did not seem to remember her son. Alone with her in her room, I told her that our father—her husband, Dalton Guy DeGresse—had met his death.

To which she said the most peculiar thing: "Did he die of madness?"

"No," I said.

"Will I?"

My whisper was barely audible: "I do not know."

She smiled a broken smile.

"Things keep falling out of the sky," she said.

I had to leave the room. My Lucas and I returned to Sweet River.

I open the letter.

Aunt Julia trusts that I am well; she does not mention my Lucas. She does, however, allude to her aging housekeeper, "Marie," from the island of Haiti and that Marie has adopted her granddaughter, "Liana," the girl having been left homeless after her parents and siblings were killed in the devastating earthquake earlier this year. Mother, Aunt Julia, Marie, and Liana have been getting by as well as possible in these economically hard times.

I stop reading.

Something is coming—I can hear it in her voice.

Aunt Julia writes that she herself is ill. Cancer.

She is dying. She has perhaps only a few months to live.

My stomach knots up.

She wants me to think about what will happen to mother and to Marie and Liana when the inevitable occurs. She writes that she has asked mother to think about where she wants to be—where she will want to end her days.

I am trembling.

I envision mother returning to this property, joining our father to haunt me to my grave.

And I would not blame them.

I deserve to have darkness in my blood.

I finish reading the letter.

I feel like writing back immediately, but I cannot.

What could I say? I shall write some other day.

I fear. I fear.

In the distant forest of my apprehensions, I think of Emily Dickinson.

This is my letter to the World
That never wrote to Me—

Perhaps this journal is my letter to the world. Perhaps it is addressed only to myself and one other.

I cringe. I tighten my body and close my eyes.

I see a small, dark creature up ahead waiting for me.

Almost a girl.

June 11

I like things with shells.

Turtles, snails, crayfish, and, despite their being as ugly as rotting toadstools, I even like armadillos. Alabama is literally teeming with those armored critters.

What kind of shell do I have?

Well, some days the cabin is my shell.

This morning, for example, I have pulled in my head, hiding from the future, from all that Aunt Julia's letter portends.

Perry Ellis stops by for coffee on his way over to Deep Kill Creek where he plans to fish for mud cats. He carries a splintered rod and reel over one shoulder; he totes a lard can of nightcrawlers for bait.

"Y'all be readin' a story tonight?"

His tone is surprisingly hopeful.

"I believe I shall. I have been thinking about Hawthorne."

"He write 'bout buryin' peoples?"

I pause. Shake my head.

"The eternal mystery of humankind—that is his common theme."

He nods. His eyes roll.

"That bad words girl comin'?"

I shrug.

"Who can say. She is a feather for each wind that blows."

"Dat what dis Hawthorne man write?"

"No. William Shakespeare. But I forget which play."

Perry Ellis leaves, promising to share his catch. He adds that he has been praying for my Lucas. I suppose it cannot hurt.

Less than an hour later I am taken aback by the arrival of
Cavatina.

"Oh, hell," she says, "here I am again."

She laughs out of congested lungs and coughs a smoker's
cough. She is wearing sweat pants and a thin top and, I believe,
one of those sport bras that plaster the breasts against the ribs
so that they will not bounce and jostle when a female runs.

But what is this young woman running from?

"I am pleased to see you," I say.

"No shit? Just wudn't sure my ass'd be welcome."

"Yes, your … Yes, you are among my most pleasant visitors."

Strangely, I realize that I am genuinely glad to see her.

"Hey, gotta ask you somethin'."

I stiffen, for I would rather not be the target of her questions
about my sexuality.

"What is it?"

"My sister, you know—Allegra. You see, she's been kinda
gettin' better, and so, well, Jesus, my God damn mother has sorta
put me in charge of her, and what I'm thinkin' is, you know, that
I'll bring her out here one of these days if it's cool with you."

Doubt rumples her pretty face. She expects me to tell her it
is probably not a good idea. For a dark moment—and I cannot
put my finger on why—I sense that it *is* a bad idea. It just feels
wrong. I bury the brief desire to protest.

"No, of course, if she wants to come."

"Oh, that's super."

Cavatina takes me up on my offer of iced tea. I lose count of
how many spoons of raw sugar she stirs into it.

"I like it kinda sweet," she says. Then, under her breath:
"Like sex." She giggles.

"I am sure that is true," I say, beside myself to figure how
this lovely young woman evolved into such a crude denizen
and, perhaps further, how it is that I have allowed her in my
cabin. And how it is that I like her.

"Hey," she follows, "since you were a teacher, could you,
you know, teach me about the woods and all?"

Her request surprises me.

What she apparently wants is to have various plants

identified, and so we strike out on one of my paths with Marauder and Jacob in tow. It is warm and sunny. I hand Cavatina an apple to give to Jacob.

"Oh, Jesus, he likes it." When she pats his neck, she issues something like a moan. "Man, dudn't he feel sexy? Shit, he is one fuckin' sexy animal."

"I have," I say, "never thought of Jacob in that way."

But then again, I admit to myself there is a quality about that mule, a muscular strength, a mysterious sensuality or sensuousness that invites one to surrender—I am speaking opaquely, of course.

In our lesson for the day, I point out the following to Cavatina: devil's walking stick—she manages to stab herself on one of the thorns even after I prompted her to be careful—chokeberry, dwarf paw paw, beautyberry, sweetshrub, oakleaf hydrangea, farkleberry, several varieties of holly as well as several varieties of fern, including Christmas fern, my favorite.

After the lesson, Cavatina takes off, vowing to return that evening.

I fix my Lucas some lunch. He eats little. I ask him to come hear Hawthorne this evening. He nods, but who knows what that means. I hope he will attend my reading—I need to have his presence close.

Thankfully the afternoon passes quickly. In preparation for the evening, I pop popcorn, though it does not pop evenly on my wood stove. I chill some wine. I put the bottle tree in place. I get the fire pit going.

I wait eagerly for my Good Faces. Yes, I have given them a name.

When they arrive, I feel a quiet elation, especially because my Lucas has come.

With everyone settled in, I say, "What is required to make us altogether human? That is the question posed by Nathaniel Hawthorne in 'Feathertop,' a tale that I personally believe is his best."

Even Perry Ellis takes the marijuana Cavatina offers tonight; he coughs with each puff, his eyes watering, Cavatina and my Lucas laughing at him—I inwardly condemn myself as a thoroughly irresponsible, reprehensible adult to allow such goings on. But then again, I do not care, for I love our little gathering, and I am not convinced that we are sinning—breaking some laws, yes; sinning, no.

My companions listen to the witchy words and deeds of Mother Rigby and, with the help of her invisible familiar, Dickon, her creation of a scarecrow, Feathertop, and his adventures in town. The alchemy of magnetic potency and the mystical drifts out from the pages. The tale flows from my lips. The wine chortles within me. I like the sound of popcorn being munched. All feels right with the world.

Too soon the story reaches an end.

Perry Ellis asks, "What done really happened to dat Feathertop? Demons get 'im?"

I hesitate for dramatic effect, and then I say, "He is like those of us who find that the world is too big—too empty and heartless. We need love to be altogether human."

Cavatina is tipsy, I believe. "That's deep shit," she exclaims. And after a few seconds in which we each muse secretly, she adds, "Hey, I got it. Oh, fuck, yes. We'll make us a God damn scarecrow. It'll keep away the Beast."

I automatically glance at my Lucas; his chest is heaving. He stands up and, rifle in hand, falls away into the night. Perry Ellis follows, his blackness both a literal and figurative shadow for the man I love.

Mention of the Beast has apparently sounded an alarm.

Watching them track away, Cavatina says, "You think your brother'll sing for us some night?"

I do not answer because I am suddenly drawn away, to the darkness of the woods where I see fireflies, lightning bugs, and yet something else, something more: what I imagine is a dark-skinned little girl lost out there and waiting. Waiting for what?

For me to rescue her?

Cavatina rattles on about how she will come back tomorrow to build a scarecrow; I nod absently. I see the firefly eyes of a child—and now I imagine that she is seeking what I am seeking—and I shudder.

Talking to herself, Cavatina steals away.

I should have insisted that she spend the night.

I go to bed. I sleep fitfully. I get up.

I make certain that the fire pit is out, and then I stare into the darkness of the woods, and something within me forces me to shout, in a voice that seems both toneless and haunting:

"Who's there?"

June 12

There are voices in my blood, but I ignore them.

    One day I shall be prepared to listen.

I take a walk over to the pond and watch the morning mist rise from the elegant surface. It is so quiet and peaceful that I wince, a privileged gesture. I begin to think about all that one naturally hopes for and all that one naturally dreads.

I think of a Dickinson poem:

Silence is all we dread.

There's Ransom in a Voice.

But Silence is Infinity.

Himself have not a face.

An icy fingernail of fear rakes down my back; I look around: where have Marauder and Jacob gone? Is someone watching? The ghost of our father? No, but I imagine a tall young man with a strong yet graceful body. And no face.

He cannot see to see.

Just my imagination, of course.

Mid-morning, Cavatina arrives with a large, plastic trash bag jammed with who knows what slung over her shoulder. Almost at the same time, Perry Ellis shows up. Have they planned something? What is afoot? It is already approaching ninety degrees.

"All right if we put up a scarecrow?" says Cavatina.

"You must have been inspired by Hawthorne," I say.

"Damn straight—cool story. Perry Ellis and me, we'll keep the Beast away from your cabin."

I laugh softly, nervously.

I sit in my Wal-Mart chair and watch. The two of them are

little more than ludic children, Perry Ellis shirtless and sweaty even before he has worked; Cavatina moves with a sexuality that is as human and necessary to her as breathing.

They choose a spot some twenty yards in front of the cabin near one of the many narrow rills that deliver run-off water to Deep Kill Creek when rains come. This particular rill is coated with moss that vibrates with a green the texture of velvet.

I sip at iced tea. The scarecrow materializes within a cloud of laughter generated by the two builders. They work quickly. Cavatina directs Perry Ellis; his fingers know the shape of fantasies and fictions.

Here is what they create: something shocking; something vaguely sacrilegious, though Perry Ellis apparently does not find the outline of it to be so. It is a figure tied to a cross, a soccer ball for a head with thick, gray, mop-head threads for hair; at first, there is no face, and I think again of Dickinson, but then Cavatina rights the situation with a black marker—eerie, triangle eyes emerge, a grisly, toothy, slash of a smile. The body is draped in a black gown, rather like a graduation gown, only the gown has a hood that mostly covers the mopish hair.

I am not surprised to see that the scarecrow is a she and that Cavatina has given it a prominent bosom—made of what, I am not sure—and has forced Perry Ellis to grope at said part of the anatomy. Grinning, he does. And then Cavatina and her partner whittle willow branches into sharp arrows—and begin to pierce the chest of the inanimate female. I see, then, that our scarecrow is quite pregnant, the womb another soccer ball.

I shake my head.

I whisper, "Gracious goodness."

The figure's arms are extended and tied to wooden cross-bars in crucifixion style. Hanging over one end is a ring comprised of devil's walking stick and snippets of briars; all in all, it appears to be a crown of thorns. Over the other end hangs a loop of new rope.

Mystery within enigma. Enigma within mystery.

I walk out from the cabin to inspect their work.

Cavatina sees me and says, "What'd ya think? Pretty damn cool, huh?"

The figure looks curiously like the Madonna—a pregnant virgin—or, with the Saint Sebastian arrows stuck into it, like a martyr of some kind.

"It should frighten Marauder and Jacob," I say. "Perhaps the Beast as well."

"And a whole lot of dem demons," Perry Ellis adds.

He is smiling; Cavatina goes to him and kisses him on the cheek. She looks back my way and giggles. "Couldn't have done it, you know, without my helper here."

Suddenly, seeing her close to Perry Ellis, I am afraid, very afraid. But of what?

"Miss DeGresse," he says, "what we gone name dis here scarecrow?"

Cavatina pipes in: "I like 'Mad Mary'—you know, she looks like the Virgin Mary stoned outta her mind."

"No, she don't," Perry Ellis counters. "She's taken on sufferin' an' demons an' defeated 'em. She be a saint is what I say."

"Shit, you can't *see* what she is," says Cavatina.

"I can *feel* what she be—I done knowed she be a saint."

I interrupt them to say, "I believe a name has occurred to me: let us call her 'Resurrection Fern.'"

For a moment, the two of them are silent. Then I see a smile spread across the face of Perry Ellis.

Cavatina shrieks, "Oh, that's so-o-o cool! So fucking cool!"

Perry Ellis agrees.

Resurrection Fern it is.

The three of us study the new creation, but not for long. Cavatina announces that she is hot and sweaty and needs a dip in the pond. She grabs the hand of Perry Ellis and drags him in that direction. He does not resist much.

I go inside for a second glass of iced tea.

Then I walk up close—not *too* close—to the scarecrow and imagine a Hawthorne fiction in which I begin to hear a beating heart, and I see the figure, resurrected, step down from the cross, seek the cool air of my kitchen and demand something to drink. Or perhaps even that I become her disciple.

I can hear Cavatina and Perry Ellis splashing in the pond.

I need to start preparing lunch for my Lucas.

I decide that Resurrection Fern is a holy horror.

But I shall let her stay.

I have also decided this: Cavatina is wicked. Or else deranged.

I do not know why I am growing to love her.

June 13

The saddest sadness is that which is not heard.

But terror often grows from a loud, seemingly source-less sound that rattles your senses—such a sound I experienced after midnight. At first, I honestly imagined that I had heard Resurrection Fern scream, a Hawthornian scream having coalesced from all of his women characters who transcend everyday reality and are punished for doing so.

I threw on my walking outfit: long-sleeved shirt, coveralls, and trekking boots. Instinctively, I grabbed my double-bladed hatchet and my flashlight. Marauder was barking a frightened bark. Jacob was snorting, one eye aflame with fear. Neither would accompany me as I struck out on one of my paths. The only thing I could determine immediately was that Resurrection Fern had not issued a peep, not even a prayer. I sprayed her with light, and I cringed. Why had I let Cavatina and Perry Ellis construct such an unsettling thing?

I did not know it then, but in the days to come, the appearance of Resurrection Fern would morph almost daily: the circle of thorns would be replaced by Mardi Gras beads on one occasion, handcuffs on another. She would don many different hats atop her black hood: a straw hat, a cowboy hat, and an extravagant number that included a crow's feather—it was a hat from some grotesque Easter parade, I assumed. One night Our Lady of the Scarecrow even wore a football helmet. Once or twice a cigarette dangled from the gash that served as her lips, but always the loop of rope remained. When I asked Cavatina about its significance, she said, "We have to have it to tie her down if she needs it done." My Lucas had glimpsed our scarecrow once, and I believe he found her troubling. "The Hawthorne story brought this on," I explained to him.

Our mother-to-be on the edge of madness and pregnant with possibilities survived thunderstorms, wind, and oppressive humidity. I planned one day to tell Cavatina and Perry Ellis that the name "Resurrection Fern" derived from that of an epiphytic plant of the fern family, one that attaches itself to both hardwoods and evergreens, and though it might appear to be a ball of brown death, it will spring to life with a good rain.

What had been something like a scream became something like a howl.

I cannot describe how awful it sounded.

As I hurried in its direction—somewhere beyond the pond—I tried to sense whether the ghost of our father lurked nearby. And what about that little girl with firefly eyes? No, of course, I had only imagined them. The howl was real, but the ghosts, I reasoned, were not.

The howls led to the rear entrance to Cat Bells.

And then I knew.

The emotions-numbing sound could only be coming from my Lucas.

I cannot for the life of me recall crawling through the opening, a maw of darkness hardly bigger around than the rim of a bushel peach basket. So concentrated was I on finding my Lucas that I pushed through my fears of the place and felt oddly relieved to be greeted by cool, somewhat moist air.

Once I had entered, the howling ceased.

I thought that, deeper in the labyrinth of the cave, I could hear the skittery chatter of bats. And then I heard sobbing.

"My Lucas!" I called out. "Sweetheart, where are you?"

I crawled several yards on my hands and knees, then rounded a blondish-colored stalagmite and swung my light off to the left. And there he was, sitting with his back against a wall, his knees rucked up, and his rifle resting next to him on the floor as if useless.

"Sweetheart, what is it? You were howling like a wolf. It scared ..."

His eyes met mine, and yet he was not seeing me. He was

seeing, once again, something lodged in his recent memory. Had he seen the Beast? What kind of blindness-not-blindness had he fallen into? Was he still falling?

Could I catch him?

Scooting up close to him, I entered the circle of his fear. He shivered and trembled, mucous running in gentle trails from his nostrils. I hugged him, and he hugged back so forcefully that I heard my bones groan and crackle.

I talked softly. Mostly I do not remember what I said except for a final question:

"Do you want to come on home?"

As he nodded, the little boy look in his eyes was crushing to me.

Back at the cabin, I gave him water; he was very thirsty. Because he seemed chilled, I set up the cot and put a heavy blanket over him. He quite suddenly seemed exhausted. He closed his eyes. I knelt beside the cot and listened.

I could barely hear him breathe.

Then I whispered, "I love you with all my heart."

Near dawn, I woke and went to check on him, but like Cavatina a few days earlier, he had gone.

I had not heard him leave.

I had not heard the depth of his sadness or whether he had reached the bottom of it.

June 14

It is a brutally humid morning.

I cannot sleep, haunted as I am by my Lucas and the horrors he is experiencing. I long to go to his trailer, and I would, but I reason that he needs his rest.

I brew coffee. I think of Whitman and the word "consolatory." From my bookshelves, I retrieve a volume entitled, *Walt Whitman's Civil War*, a mosaic of materials, including letters and poems centered on the great poet's days as a nurse, secular chaplain, and hospital volunteer in Washington. Whitman termed himself a "visitor & consolatory." The latter is a lovely word—I fear, however, that the terrible war blasted the good man—just as the Beast has blasted my Lucas.

I wish to be my brother's consolatory. And more.

I sit out by my fire pit and nearly doze off.

Singing a hymn, Perry Ellis is trundling towards the cabin, and though the pull to go to my Lucas continues to be strong, I greet my visitor instead.

"Good morning, preacher man," I say.

He smiles a broad, pleased-to-be-alive smile.

"Y'all see what's 'round Miss Fern's neck?"

I glance over at the scarecrow. Good heavens. She is wearing a poster board with words printed in black marker. It reads as follows:

NO JESUS
NO PEACE
KNOW JESUS
KNOW PEACE

Why, I wonder, is Christianity so given to triteness and

banality? I caution myself to be polite.

"Whose handiwork is it?"

"The bad words girl," he says. "She done write it up for me."

"Her name is 'Cavatina.'"

"Yessum—'Calf-uh-tima.'"

"Oh, Perry Ellis, you are not trying."

He pauses. Nods. Squints in my direction.

"She be my friend."

And something comes over me. A twitch of dismay or perhaps even anger. I can feel my jaw stiffen.

"I do not think you should spend so much time with her."

He pauses even longer this time.

"Why dat?"

"Because."

I am holding back a flood of things. I want to teach him that the wild girl he calls his friend is profane, vulgar, masochistic, immoral, and vile. I want to demand that he not go swimming naked with her in the pond. Mostly, I do not even want to talk about Cavatina; I want to ask him about my Lucas, about what happens to him on his nocturnal rambles.

"All right den," he says, "I'm guessin' I'm gone on to catch some fish. Bound to have better luck today."

Exasperated, I say, "You do not even have your pole or bait."

He shrugs and drifts away.

I want to call him back and apologize. Instead, I decide to escape the heat. And that is when I see it: a note tacked to the front door. I take it down and seek out the shadowy coolness of my kitchen. My hands are quivering. I recognize the boyish scrawl immediately.

"Jessica Love—do not leave the cabin today. The Beast has mutinied against the command of all that lives. You are in danger. Be alone. I will protect Lucas."

My heart is beating so rapidly that I have trouble breathing. I read the note twice more. My thoughts scatter. My Lucas has always called me "Jessica Love" because he could not, I assumed, pronounce "Lovelia." The word "mutinied" is curious, and what on earth is "the command of all that lives?" And

I am struck, of course, by the unintentional irony of his closing. I am quite certain that he meant to place a comma after "protect"—truth is, though, my Lucas is most definitely the one most in need of protection.

I am both frightened and touched by the note.

I obey.

All morning and into the warm afternoon I lose myself in Whitman. I do not leave the cabin. I notice that Marauder and Jacob stay close as well. Do they know something I do not? After a light lunch I grow drowsy. I lie down on the cot; I can smell my Lucas. I look again at his note, tracing my fingers over each letter, each word.

I fall asleep, and the dream I have is brief, yet electrifying: almost a vision, it is of something white, like an angel, but more earthly than heavenly. I see it in the woods; it transforms into a walking corpse moving away from me at first—then it glances over its shoulder and buries its eyes in me. It is a hideous thing. Was it our father? No, more like a malicious stranger.

I jerk awake as if scalded. Then I feel cold in the shadows. Out of nowhere comes a remembrance of a poem by Wallace Stevens entitled, "The Snow Man." I wish that I had a mind of winter, but I do not. Groggy minutes pass. I fall asleep again only to experience an even more terrifying dream: that I have been buried alive. For what seems an eternity, I cannot move. I can hear something brushing against my kitchen window, something large and dark and unrevealable. I cannot scream. I cannot free myself to get my hatchet. As I watch the window, a huge head swings into view—I am sure it must be the Beast. I tense every muscle in my body. The head of whatever it is tilts; a single eye constellates with an indifferent glint.

It is Jacob.

My paralysis relents. Angry, shaken, I go to the window and shoo him away. I grit my teeth. I stagger around my kitchen thoroughly enervated. But then I listen. I think it has become late afternoon. I have lost track of time. I hear a strange noise— an odd whistling, followed by what I can only describe as a grinding scream. I imagine dead souls wailing and begging for mercy.

Then it evaporates.

Silence reigns.

I sit at my table and bury my face in my hands.

How much time elapses I cannot say. Eventually I am startled by a knocking at the door. It is my Lucas. Overjoyed, I go to him and collapse into his arms. In something of a drunken dance, we inch back to the table. I look at him. His eyes have been burned by fear, reamed out by fingers of terror. He has not slept. His mind is an out-of-control fire.

I give him cold water. His thirst is immense.

The fire in his mind appears to lessen significantly.

I tell him about my dreams, my visions.

"What did I see? That man, a stranger, not our father—was it the Beast?"

My Lucas is now alert; he gestures for paper and something to write with. He writes slowly, almost painfully. I read his response:

"You saw a woman white as snow."

I know that he cannot be right.

I interrogate him, but he writes nothing more.

I think of a white goddess. I imagine Resurrection Fern draped in white. I imagine a sphinx with breasts as large as Cavatina's.

My Lucas, more dead than alive, rises and slips into what remains of the day.

Who, I wonder, will save him now?

For I cannot.

June 15

What strange gods have brought me to this wild incompletion? I am sitting in front of the cabin beholding first light and talking aloud to myself and being overheard by Marauder, Jacob, and Resurrection Fern. I look into the woods, and I think of a partial line from Whitman's "Song of Myself": *My voice goes after what my eyes cannot reach....*

The humid morning air attempts to squash my body.

My body.

Is it composing a song of *myself*?

Off in the direction of my brother's trailer, I hear the backfire of a truck—it is not that of a familiar vehicle. Not the one belonging to my Lucas. My brain tenses. My heart flutters.

I want the intimate, surrounding spaces to mother me.

Someone is approaching the cabin. Marauder barks, and a man's voice, soft yet commanding, shushes my sentry, and then I hear, "Miss DeGresse—y'all be 'bout?"

First I see my Lucas. Dark heavens! He looks awful, almost alive. His eyes hold on desperately to extreme fear as if he is about to drop into an unpeopled abyss where something beyond fear lurks. Naked from the waist up, he flinches, seemingly at noises echoing within him; he possesses no more spirit than ... than a scarecrow. His skin evidences deep scratches as if he has been attacked by one or more of those demons Perry Ellis senses in the everywhere. He is wet and muddy and, even at some distance, smells of swamp stink.

"Yes, I am here," I call out as Tobias Bonnard—"T-Bone"— and my Lucas approach like a man and his prisoner of war. "Oh, what has happened to him?"

Mr. Bonnard has deep sadness and concern in his tone. He places a meaty hand, shaped rather like a starfish, on the shoulder of my Lucas.

"I found him jus' 'fore dawn. Heard him howlin' and cryin'. He was thrashin' 'round in the swamp—lost he was and hurtin'. I thought it be best if I brung him to y'all."

"Thank you, Mr. Bonnard. Thank you, sir."

Mr. Bonnard smiles shyly and touches the bill of his greasy, sweat-stained baseball cap. He is a hulk of a man, large the way a massive boar is large, with a pronounced stomach. His arms are round and beaten red, but I know that they are strong. Behind his black-rimmed glasses, his eyes are bloodshot and tiny, a pig's eye dullness there. His face is red and splotchy, and his graying, thin growth of beard is more bristles than hair. Beneath his overalls, he wears a dun-colored T-shirt, short-sleeved. His boots might have been borrowed from a fairy tale ogre.

"He done needs attention, ma'am."

We take him inside. Mr. Bonnard helps me remove my brother's jeans and boots. We lift him onto my bed.

"There, sweetheart," I say. "You rest. Just rest."

His eyes roll. His tongue clicks as if he wants or needs to speak. Then he shivers as if the room has a temperature below zero. I reach out to soothe his face with my fingertips, and he hisses at me like a cornered animal.

I pitch backward and watch as he rolls over and begins, with difficulty, to sleep.

Silent tears course down my face.

I stagger into the kitchen on the heels of my brother's savior. Mr. Bonnard and I sit at my table, and he says, "I give him plenty uh water. Them scratches will done need tendin'."

I agree.

But I am thinking: my Lucas cannot live. He cannot live. It is impossible for him to live his life. He is beyond his own departing.

"Thank you," I say tonelessly.

"He wudn't far from my tavern, Miss DeGresse. Like I said, he was hurtin' and lost, and he done talked some, but what he is said done made not a lick uh sense."

I stare at Mr. Bonnard.

"My Lucas spoke?"

"Yes, ma'am. Like uh dead man done would have." Then he ducks his head away and plays his fingers nervously together. "I'm thinkin' maybe he needs to see one uh them doctors that help men get over the war—get shet uh the things they've seen."

"He has," I say. "He has been to the vet clinic people in Tuskegee and Montgomery both. They do not seem to be able to help him. I thought maybe *I* could."

"Yes, ma'am. Well, he sure 'nuf needs … well, it's like probably I don't know what he done needs."

I am stuck upon a question. Nothing else seems to matter.

"What did he say to you? You see, he has not spoken a word to me for several months."

Mr. Bonnard removes his cap and rubs at his scalp. Then issues a half chuckle of bewilderment, or so it appears.

"Crazy things, mainly. Well, he done said he'd been followin' uh woman. Like uh vision uv'uh woman. She was dressed in white. Said he heard violin music, beautiful music—God's truth, that's what he done said. The music came outter her like outter uh radio—that's what he done said. And he told me that some kinda animal led him to this here woman." He pauses, shakes his head, wipes at the moisture on his lips.

I offer him some iced tea.

I tell him about the Beast.

I say, "I fear that my Lucas believes he must slay the Beast to live again—to be born anew."

He waggles his head, a man befuddled.

"All right then," he says. "That's hard for uh man like myself to understand. Your daddy, he done had some strange thoughts 'bout the swamp and 'bout your land here. I jus' don't know."

He drinks a full glass of iced tea right down to the bottom. His pink face beads sweat.

"If the Beast truly exists," I say, "what is it, and do you believe it necessarily intends to do harm?"

I find myself holding my breath as I wait a long run of seconds for his response.

"There's mysteries in these parts—I done knowed that for uh fact. Could be some kinda creature nobody really knowed. But if there is, no, ma'am, I 'spect it don't want to hurt 'cept when it gots to eat. I 'spect it jus' wants to live and be left alone."

I think of *Moby Dick*. I smile to myself. Mr. Bonnard likely assumes I am going strange.

"Ahab was compelled by a force beyond his control—that is my Lucas as well. I wish he would not listen to ghosts."

Mr. Bonnard's mouth falls open. His lips move like a carp feeding in the pond.

"Yes, ma'am."

I thank him once again, and when he asks what else he can do to help, I say, "I could use a fresh supply of your wonderful wine."

He smiles and touches the bill of his cap. As he is leaving, he turns; the bulk of his body appears to shrink with a self-effacing timidity.

"How is your mama doin' these days?"

"She is much the same as always."

"Please tell her I've done been uh thinkin' 'bout her from time to time." His eyes swing away, then he lowers his chin and mumbles something I probably am not meant to hear: "I sure do miss her."

Why, oh why I say what I say next is a genuine mystery to me.

"It might could be she will be coming back to stay before too long."

Hearing my words, his body seems to regain its size. He nods. He steps out onto my path with amazing agility for a large man. He moves younger than his age. Then he turns and tugs at the bill of his cap in a gesture of goodbye.

Perhaps he is also thanking me for the secret language of hope. If so, he trusts words more than I do.

My Lucas sleeps through lunch; he sleeps through the afternoon. I bathe every inch of his body in cool water. He stirs and groans. I medicate the wounds to his flesh; I can only speculate about the wounds to his psyche.

I lie down on the bed and curl up close to him.

He smells distant from life, but I love him. He rests as profoundly as Sleeping Beauty. He has not lived in many months, asleep in some realm unknown to me. Has someone cast a spell upon him?

I kiss his lips.

He does not awaken.

The woods bake. The temperature soars well into the nineties. A brief rain shower drenches the property—humidity then closes in like a predator.

I merely cope.

Twilight arrives.

I fix my Lucas a cup of chicken broth. He drinks some of it before returning to his ongoing nightmare where I assume he is pursuing phantoms and being pursued by them.

I am restless.

I build flames in my fire pit and try to relax with my volumes of Poe and Dickinson. Around sunset, Mr. Bonnard returned with twenty bottles or so of his wine. I put several of them in a tub of ice. I thanked Mr. Bonnard still again for helping my Lucas. A studied joy held his expression in place.

"I done thought uh your mama—how she'd be pleased if somebody saw to her boy."

I did not, of course, tell him that mother no longer even recognizes her son.

Shadows thicken as the fire pit flames leap and dance. Sparks escape. And for some reason I set out the bottle tree. Marauder flops down away from the fire pit and pants into the evening's heat. I can hear Jacob stamp his hooves and swish his tail at biting insects, but I cannot see his eyes. I glance in the direction of Resurrection Fern, and I stifle a shriek: there is a lighted candle resting atop her head. Who on earth placed it there? The small flame flickers, and I imagine the flaming eyes of a child off deep in the woods—from whence comes that image? It puzzles me.

"Hey dare, Miss DeGresse."

I wheel about.

"Good heavenly days," I exclaim. "You like to scared the life out of me, Perry Ellis. Could you please announce yourself? You might have been stealing up on me to cut my throat."

He smiles broadly, teeth glistening white.

"Y'all gone be readin' tonight?"

"Perhaps."

There is a slight breeze. I know he can hear the bottle tree clinking. He pets Marauder and whistle-chirps at Jacob. He is a young man on the cusp of contentment.

We visit a few minutes before we hear voices on the main path. We see the beam of a flashlight. It is Cavatina, her firm, full breasts threatening to spill out of her flimsy top.

She has someone with her.

I see a flash of white. My breath catches.

"You guys," says Cavatina, "hey, shit, look at this—I brought my older sister. This is 'Allegra.'"

Over the years, I have come to believe that our lives have *turnings*, moments in which the mystical journey we are on forks off in an unexpected way. Meeting Allegra is going to be one of them.

I feel it.

We all engage in introductions.

And then I drink in this curious young woman, more than a girl. I apply all my powers of perception, and this is what I read of her:

She is taller, less buxom than Cavatina. Her reddish hair curls limply at her shoulders. Her face is pale, freckled somewhat—a subtle beauty resides there on her cheeks, the shape of her lips and nose and eyebrows, and the longer I look the more curiously strange her loveliness becomes. Everything centers on her eyes. Everything begins and ends with them. As with her body, her eyes seem poorly fed, and yet I have never seen such intensity in human eyes. Such expectation. Her eyes signal a preternatural alertness as if she is waiting, anticipating at every instant that something or someone will appear to warrant her brilliant focus.

What is she expecting to find here? I ask myself.

I fear her without knowing why.

I sense that she dreams awake.

I know that I will either love her or hate her.

I blink and peruse her further. She wears cargo pants and canvas shoes, but what dominates her attire is a short, terrycloth bathrobe belted at the waist—it is white. As white as a vision.

Cavatina jokes about it: "Fuckin' weird, huh? She just loves that old robe. Wears it fuckin' everywhere, you know."

Allegra smiles demurely; my heart pounds like a kettle drum. I think this: Allegra lives in neverness. Cavatina lives nearby. We sit.

Allegra, a wisp of nothingness, speaks in a voice that leaves no trace. She casts a shadow that no other human being casts—odd that such a quietly ridiculous observation enters my consciousness.

Cavatina asks about my Lucas.

I ramble. I say too much, and scold myself. My eyes start to tear up. I stop somewhere mid-sentence; silence pours in and around us before Perry Ellis says, "Darkness, hit knows Mr. Lucas."

Allegra follows, her hands clasped as if she is in a waiting room of some kind. Her voice is that of someone coming suddenly out of a coma.

"He must be wonderful," she says.

I nod.

Cavatina grins her endemically wicked grin. Searches me with her naked eyes.

"You don't talk about him like you're his brother—fucking strange."

I shoot her a disapproving frown. Then I offer wine, and the scene—a slightly different gathering of Good Faces—softens, and Perry Ellis asks me to read to them.

I open the pages of my friend, Miss Emily, the woman of white heat verse, and my voice flows from the life of my spirit, not my body.

A Death blow is a Life blow to Some
Who till they died, did not alive become—
Who had they lived—had died but when
They died, Vitality begun—

I stop. "I am truly sorry," I say.

For the poem now seems to me to cruelly target Allegra—what she has gone through.

"What the fuck?" says Cavatina.

Stephen Gresham

Perry Ellis has a stampede of confusion in his expression.

Allegra turns into my eyes; her voice is now like song:

"My life got buried—not my death—it's swimming in this river of night."

It is a lyrical gesture of forgiveness.

And I want to exclaim to my young listeners that life is all about drives, the will, passions—being wanted, needed. Life is filled with equal parts poetry and poison. Seek the poetry; be wary wise about the poison.

I shift to Poe.

I cannot resist choosing "Spirits of the Dead."

That marvelous second stanza trips off my tongue as if the very spirit of Poe has possessed me.

Be silent in that solitude,
Which is not loneliness—for then
The spirits of the dead who stood
In life before thee are again
In death around thee—and their will
Shall overshadow thee: be still.

At the conclusion of all five stanzas, I lift my eyes melodramatically—the mystery of mysteries hangs in the air—and Perry Ellis is breathing heavily.

"Oh, fuck," Cavatina whispers.

Out of the corner of my eye I see Allegra fall away into herself. I should not, I tell myself, have chosen this particular poem, and yet the young woman is a soul alone, no need for me or the others.

And I am astonished as she intones, repeating all twenty-eight lines, every word perfectly, with as much assurance as she would speak her own name. It gives me a nasty fright. It affirms that I will not sleep well.

And I hear something more in Allegra's performance.

Hers is the voice of one who will not die.

June 16

Iam gazing into a future that refuses to come into focus. I do
not have the right eyes to see what cannot be seen. Things are
falling from sight.

June 17

My Lucas cannot wake into his life.
    Night has risen.

I stand naked before my mirror—not the fairest in the land.
Candles flicker.

I am shrinking. Growing darker. I am becoming a shadow
of my shadow.

June 18

This approaches the hottest June I can recall.

Although the cabin is canopied by leafy hardwoods and holds cooler air within for many hours of daylight, the heat saps me. My Lucas sleeps as if he cannot choose otherwise. I bathe him occasionally with cold water, but I am running low on ice. I may have to ask Perry Ellis to fetch me some. When my Lucas surfaces to almost full consciousness, I feed him soft foods. He seems to like small chunks of watermelon, so sweet and easy to swallow. When he surrenders to sleep again, I lightly kiss away the sticky seepings around his mouth. He never knows.

I have no visitors.

Late afternoon, the heat a furnace blast one cannot resist, I strip down naked and crawl under the thin, white sheet with my Lucas. I wish that I had Cavatina's sexy body and her lascivious ways or the attractive aura of Allegra's spirit.

I want my Lucas, the weight of his body on mine.

I kiss him unaware.

My fingers tremble—for I am new to this—as I spider-walk down his stomach and reach inside his underwear and touch and touch.

He stirs gently. But he does not respond.

I sigh as if it is a death gasp.

I touch his cheek.

I touch his bare chest. Muscles. Skin. I lower my ear and listen to the beat of his heart, the *da-dunt, da-dunt* seems to come from down in the cave of his ribs. When his body shifts, the beat grows faint. He snores lightly. Turns away.

I touch his back.

I pull my hand away.

And I touch myself.

Strokes. Stroking. Swallowing tiny cups filled with desire.

Stroking until the darkened room sparkles with surges of pleasure, glitters with the pulsing of something primitive in the blood.

Almost satisfaction.

On shaky legs, I leave my bed and my Lucas.

I wash my hands.

I shall not condemn myself for allowing my love for my Lucas to become lust. I shall not.

I build a modest fire in my hearth, for my naked skin goose bumps with the chill of cooling passion. I sit and gaze into the indifferent flames. I feel little warmth.

My imagination is insistent: soon my seven literary companions—my tribe—join me; they seem not to notice or care that I am not wearing clothing. My spirit is adorned with rags, comfortable, familiar lendings. And I wonder: if my favorite writers were real and present, how would they feel about my so-called sinful longings for my brother?

Dickinson—my white, yearning flame that is Emily, strong poetess—she would understand, I believe. She would sort me out.

Whitman? Mr. Walt—oh, he would smilingly applaud, would he not? He the man who loves *all* his brothers and whenever possible. And he would sing of my conflicted audacity.

Melville's agnostic being might be confused into knowing.

Hawthorne would bid me to look into my own heart—do you see darkness or light?

Poe—Emerson's jingle man—would encourage me to listen when my demons speak—listen well.

Emerson and Thoreau—oh, the latter might ask me if I were following the path of my fate. His sometimes friend, Mr. Ralph, I think would have the best response of any: *do not let yourself become diminished*—no answer at all, perhaps, and yet words I would clasp to my bosom as if I understood perfectly.

But do I truly know their thoughts? I am no scholar of these greats. I am certainly no poet. I have little wisdom. No song. But

I am a reader. My faithful seven reside faithfully in the endless book of my imagination. Alas, I have almost nothing original to say. I fear, in fact, that many of my journal entries are shabby plagiarisms. Shameful borrowings. Am I too lazy a writer to be precise?

As usual at such moments, Solitude is here costumed like Karloff as the creature, alone in a far corner, his face half in shadow, the other half abandoned. And Madness, she, too— looking, no surprise, much too much like my mother. Why is she staring at me? A mirror of her insanity?

I am tired.

This longing body, outrun by sexual desire, needs rest. I have decisions to make. And I must make them alone.

June 19

The howling of my Lucas wakes me.

Is it possible that the Beast possesses him?

He struggles to sit up in bed. I give him glasses of cold water. I mop his brow.

In the candlelight, his eyes come alive briefly, and when I swing into his focus, he growls and bares his teeth, a wolf in the memory; his face riots—fear and hatred and mystery.

I love all of him that frightens me.

When I slip out of the room, plunging it in darkness, the bestial in him subsides. I hear Marauder barking as if in terror. Jacob is braying horrors through his teeth.

I go outside and try to calm them.

Resurrection Fern cackles, or so it seems.

I sit in the oppressive humidity, in the quiet rhythms of my mystifying world, and I think about what I should do, what I *must* do.

First issue: to decide what is best for my Lucas, for Perry Ellis, Cavatina, and now Allegra—my Good Faces. I know, of course, that my Lucas needs help, specialized, professional help. He should be in a facility that can address his problems. I know this to be true: his mind is dead wild. His life is almost lost. He should not remain with me or near me and neither should the others. If I had compassion and humanity, I would send my Lucas away, and I would tell the others to stay far from here— go back to civilization and become civilized and let this lonely woman embrace her lonelitude.

Give me space to heal myself.

To forgive myself.

You see, there are those to whom I must confess—to mother for trying to drive her insane in my jealousy over the birth of my sister long ago and to our father for what I did on a cold day last January when he was having trouble breathing and, frustrated, he pulled his oxygen apparatus away from his mouth and nose, and I looked into those panicked eyes that so often abused me and I …

Some things are too difficult to trust.

Emerson strides into my thoughts: "Self-Reliance"—"Trust thyself: every heart vibrates to that iron string." But how often, for me, has that string felt like a noose? He writes, "Nothing can bring you peace but yourself." Amen, I say. And yet.

I go back inside and retrieve my volume of Emerson, and I read the following from his essay, "Circles":

"The one thing which we seek with insatiable desire is to forget ourselves, to be surprised out of our propriety, to lose our sempiternal memory, and to do something without knowing how or why; in short, to draw a new circle. Nothing great was ever achieved without enthusiasm."

Goodness, what beautiful words!

In the pages of Emerson, I feel that I belong to myself.

But then, inevitably, I close the book.

Here is what I know, with or without enthusiasm: that language fails, that Solitude is an unloved creature—even his creator abandoned him, that alone is not safe and not complete, and that the old paths spoken of in the Bible lead away from but always back to the deception of the heart.

I need the spirit-rending, lovely gathering of younger folk, not because I want to become their teacher, but because I sense that *they* are leading *me* somewhere or to someone.

My body will survive the scorching heat of this day.

My spirit will prevail if I allow it to command me.

I have to stay myself in my own shell.

The turtle will not try

Unless you leave him—then return—

And he has hauled away.

So I must "haul away" and absorb the energy of youth and my new community.

I smile at Dickinson's lines and at my own thoughts—they come from a place between the end of the universe and the merely human.

I could be very wrong in being hopeful.

Perhaps, indeed, I am the *only* fool in foolish.

Mid-afternoon, a shattering downpour. I should be frightened of such a storm—the toad-strangling rain, stabbing lightning, and hammering thunder.

But I am not.

June 20

Sunday morning.
   Father's Day.
   I suppose the ghost of our father has been sitting in my chair at my table. Yes, it is cold to the touch. If I but believed in him, I would never need ice. I would simply ask him to stir his hauntingly frigid finger in my tea or blow upon it with his breath of the Arctic.

My Lucas is up and about. His eyes, brighter now, signal that some kind of curious fever—not of the body—has broken. Yet, he remains weak, energy leaking in whispers from his muscles and bones with every movement. He saddens me deeply. But he eats a plate of breakfast: scrambled eggs, crisp bacon, and cornbread—he swallows back his former lives, or so I choose to think.

He seems defeated.

He seems resigned to a state of being that I will never understand.

Is living his life truly impossible? Why must I keep asking that?

What more can I do?

I shall read to him. And so I do.

I want suddenly to give my Lucas courage and freedom— what Emerson called "wildness." Can words accomplish that? Can poetry? Art? I shall turn to Whitman and Melville for assistance.

When, I wonder, will the river of the nightmare upon which my Lucas drifts run its course? I seek out Whitman. I believe it was Wallace Stevens who said of Mr. Walt:

"Nothing is final, he chants. No man shall see the end."

Whitman, I used to tell my classes, is the great poet of imme-diacy. Is that not what my Lucas needs?

I read the first two hundred lines or so of "Song of Myself." My Lucas listens, but I feel that he grows restless. Will he con-tinue to pursue the Beast? I put down Whitman, and I say, "Would you like for me to read you *Billy Budd*?"

My Lucas nods, Handsome Sailor in his own right.

I read Melville's great work, filling my solemn kitchen with it. My Lucas and I see the end of it—to the tragic silence of the unjust execution and beyond. I have tears in my eyes.

When I apologize to my Lucas for my flaccid surrender to emotion, he grasps my wrist and almost speaks. Our eyes meet—no deadly space between—and I love him more than any words could express.

He gestures for paper and a pencil, and he writes, "Do you hear music?"

He looks into me, seemingly desperate and very confused.

"No, sweetheart," I say.

What on earth is wrong? What is happening?

Then he closes his eyes, and I can tell that he is listening even more intensely, and perhaps he hears music from the supra-sensible realm. Is he being called?

He pushes away from the table, ducks his head shyly and leaves the cabin.

I want to cry out for him to stop. But I do not.

Lost.

Lost.

Lost.

On my life, he is lost.

June 21

It will be a long day.

Summer solstice has arrived. I feed Marauder and Jacob, and I smile at the sight of Resurrection Fern wearing sunglasses. I dredge up my Latin and consider the word "solstice"—*sol* (sun), *sistere* (stand still)—a term meant to capture perfectly that mystical moment in which the sun, in effect, stops, then begins to draw a new pattern, almost a circle, I suppose. With such thoughts, I feel much too Emersonian.

I am trying not to think about my Lucas.

I fear that I, too, have ceased living my life.

But I am resolved. Late morning, I prepare a light lunch and take it to my Lucas. I do not believe that he has been hunting the Beast. I breathe deeply because I have come to do the hardest thing—tell my Lucas that he must go away. He must seek help, medical help. We must pursue that route once more. I shall assist him, of course. I choke out the words. He will not look me in the eyes; he stares at some vanishing point beyond Nahollo Swamp. I clear my throat, and I suggest that he spend the rest of the day thinking about what I have said. Tomorrow morning we can begin our search for a good doctor and a good healing facility. We must try harder.

He does not eat his lunch.

I tell him that I love him and that I shall always, always, always love him.

He disappears inside his derelict trailer.

On my self-pitying walk back to the cabin, I follow the traces left by love. I try not to lose my way.

I sleep most of the afternoon.

As warm, evening air holds sway, Perry Ellis calls out his visitor's greeting, and I reluctantly build a fire in my fire pit. The two of us share a chilled bottle of wine.

"Perry Ellis," I say, "we are becoming winos. Will your God strike us down for our lack of sobriety?"

"He might could." Then he hesitates. He knows something. He is lousy at being deceptive. "Dem sisters be comin'." He smiles, his crooked teeth a jumble.

And I realize that I am glad Cavatina and Allegra will join us. As we wait, I tell Perry Ellis what I have decided regarding my Lucas.

"I be prayin' for 'im, Miss DeGresse."

"Thank you—I am open to things I would not normally believe."

When Cavatina and Allegra pour out of the shadows of the woods into our patch of light, our merging of fire and lantern light, I see that Allegra continues to wear her white bathrobe. I see also that she is carrying what appears to be a very small suitcase.

"Looky here," says Cavatina. "Allegra brought her fiddle."

Allegra smiles at me, and I am penetrated.

"It is my mother's violin. She no longer plays it."

"No," Cavatina intrudes. "She's never fucking sober enough to."

I invite the girls—the young women—to sit and join us, and offer them wine. Perry Ellis wants me to read Poe. He helps me set out the bottle tree. It feels good to be in the midst of youth.

Community.

"So where's that sexy fox brother of yours?"

It is Cavatina grinning, the tip of her tongue protruding with desire.

I confide in my group. I fight a rush of emotion as I explain the situation that my Lucas finds himself in. I say too much, I fear—it is a bad habit I have. When I finish, I am surprised to see Allegra coming to me, leaning down, hugging me quietly, softly. She smells like magnolia blossoms beyond their prime, and yet she smells like compassion. She confuses me: I believe that while she converses with beauty, I also sense that she has the power to call upon poisonous names. I thank her for her hug, for her concern.

I read two pieces by Poe: the first, "Silence—A Fable."

I know that it will be riveting to Perry Ellis, what with "the Demon" as a speaker. Sure enough, when I reach those final, enigmatic lines of the narrator—"And I could not laugh with the Demon, and he cursed me because I could not laugh. And the lynx which dwelleth forever in the tomb, came out there-from, and lay down at the feet of the Demon, and looked at him steadily in the face."—Perry Ellis jumps up and mutters something. He grips his corn knife; he is distraught. Cavatina embraces him, settles him with whispers, kisses him on the ear, and holds his hand.

I apologize to him.

And Allegra asks, "Did Poe ever write a romance? A love story?"

There is a ghostly alertness in her voice, one that I cannot shake.

"Yes," I say, "a tragic romance set in Venice."

"Oh, I have always wanted to go there," she follows.

I smile cautiously, and I read "The Visionary," sometimes called "The Assignation." Poe's favorite theme of the death of a beautiful lady fills the tale replete with the Byronic atmosphere of funereal gondolas and darknesses within shadows. It is a narrative of a child rescued and an illicit relationship between two doomed lovers who appear to die apart simultaneously.

"Holy shit!" Cavatina exclaims, in her accustomed manner, when I complete the story. "That was pretty damn awesome!"

Perry Ellis shakes his head. "What done happened? I don't never understand dese stories."

"My theory," I say, "is that it was a planned suicide: death by poison of both the Byronic figure and the Marchesa Aphrodite."

"I agree," says Allegra. "They die, but on the far side of our earthly reality they will share a new love, a true, spiritual love."

I glance at her. I bathe in her words. Then I quake ever so slightly because I sense that I shall never know this girl, this young woman who, in the past, rose from her own death.

The four of us talk further about Poe's story and about the

difficulties of love. A moment is ushered in—I think of my Lucas, and I turn to Allegra and ask her to play her violin. She agrees to.

"I will play from the allegro appassionato movement of Mendelssohn's famous violin concerto."

I can only report that the atmosphere surrounding our gathering is surreal—an evident portending commands each moment as Allegra fingers her instrument and begins to play.

I am carried away.

Like gipsy music that one might hear in a paradise of one's choosing.

When she strokes to a conclusion, her never-to-know-death eyes aflame with passion, we applaud. Marauder barks. Jacob neighs. Resurrection Fern seems to jangle in her shadows.

And there is more.

Not more music. More scene.

Minutes later, as we are talking and enjoying the end of earth's longest day, I hear him approach—my Lucas. When he enters to our presence, we greet him, and Allegra rises.

And I feel myself sinking away.

I watch as the eyes of my Lucas lock on to the eyes of Allegra.

Like statues, the two of them stand still.

Perfectly still.

World and mind seem one. They are alone together.

No one else matters.

I do not know—shall never know—what is passing, word-lessly, between them.

Perhaps it is as if Life and Death are staring at one another.

She who will not die has met he who cannot live.

June 22

I become exhausted by the thought: what should I do?

On my path by the pond, I look out and see soft-shelled turtles already sunning themselves on rocks this morning. They are motionless, soaking in the cosmos and apparently free of worry, comfortable in their shells. I envy them.

Our gathering last night haunts me.

I watched, helplessly, as Cavatina and Perry Ellis stole off into the shadows. I could hear them giggling. I censored my thoughts and dark projections of what they might have been doing. More alarmingly, my Lucas and Allegra strolled off together as well. I did not hear a conversation; I do not know where they went or what they did.

I should be pleased.

I should be pleased that my Lucas has responded to another human being.

I should be.

Later in the night, Cavatina and Allegra returned to the cabin and then headed off home.

I was relieved.

But this morning, I go to my brother's trailer and find the door unlocked, but he is not inside. His truck is where it always is, and so I can only speculate that he is out on patrol, hunting the Beast. Or has he left never to return?

It is twilight now.

My Lucas is nowhere to be found.

I am very worried.

Sleep will not be possible.

June 23

Because the solstice has passed, darkness will deepen each day.

It is difficult to read the innumerable pages of the future in the murky light just before dawn. So much alone, I rise and dress and walk through the dew, hoping that my Lucas has returned. But I am disappointed. Still no sign of him: his trailer is filled with clutter, and yet it seems hollow, vacant, not just empty—an empty too much.

I walk beyond the pond, following my path up to Cat Bells, and I listen for any sound or indication of him I seek. Over my shoulder, I see that Marauder and Jacob are tagging along at a respectable distance.

Has my Lucas taken his life?

The thought scalds me.

What an odd expression: "taken his life." Where has he taken it? And why? With poison?

Waiting, I feel like a caged animal.

I pace.

Back at my cabin, I see things differently. Another possibility among the inscrutable possibilities emerges: *the woman white as snow.* Now it makes sense. When my Lucas met Allegra, the girl who will not die, his was a decisive encounter with the one in his vision, the one connected to the music he claimed to hear. Of course. The white bathrobe. The violin. They went off together so that my Lucas could tell her of his curious vision and of his love for music.

Yes. And now he is somewhere grappling with the implications of this transformative meeting. He is "out there" trying to determine what it all means, the strangeness of it all. Has Allegra made him see that he must live, that he must embrace the mystery of life? Did he talk with her? He must have.

I am cheered.

Just as quickly, I am jealous, for I wonder, naturally, whether my Lucas might be attracted, in a romantic sense, to Allegra, despite the fact that he is twenty years older than she—old enough to be her father.

I brew coffee. I have no appetite for food.

I think about another woman in white: my Emily.

Had I a mighty gun

I think I'd shoot the human race.

I chuckle at Dickinson's lines—what had provoked them?

I think of how impersonal the color white is. In Poe's *The Narrative of Arthur Gordon Pym*, white is the secret theme, white evokes terror. White is anathema. And then, of course, there is *Moby Dick*, that chapter entitled, "The Whiteness of the Whale"—was it not the whale's *whiteness* that appalled Ishmael? Finally, it seems that the whale destroyed his faith in the benign aspects of whiteness.

But perhaps Allegra renewed the faith of my Lucas.

I wish suddenly that I could go an entire hour without thinking.

When Perry Ellis arrives later, he shows me what he has made for Cavatina: it is a cross and a dagger combined. It is oak, carved delicately and stained a dark and oily brown. The point of the blade, despite being hewn of wood, is very sharp.

"She will love it," I tell him.

He hopes so.

We drink coffee and talk about my Lucas, and I ask him to go to Mr. Bonnard's tavern to see whether he has seen my wayward brother.

We must find my Lucas to make certain that he finds himself.

June 24

I walk in futile spirals and many-angled rounds, covering nearly every inch of my property—the dominion of the unattained. I am so distraught that I sit on the weedy bank of Deep Kill Creek, and I converse with Marauder and Jacob as the morning heats up. No, of course, it is not conversation; it is confession. Animals are perfect confessors because they hear but do not listen. Or is it listen but do not hear?

What do I tell them?

That I cannot bear for my Lucas to suffer.

That I would rather die than lose him to otherness.

Then, as if prompted by some signal they have exchanged, Marauder and Jacob push down the bank past me, cross a sandbar and wade out into the sluggish current. I smile at the sight of them. They are in a realm beyond worry.

And so I join them.

Something here in the wet flow of Nature is waiting to be discovered.

The water, surprisingly cold, rises above my hiking boots. I wade and stomp and laugh at the thunk of splashes; I scoop handfuls of the creek and toss them at my companions, but I do not, as they, lower my mouth to drink.

My Lucas is never far from my thoughts.

I wade farther, deeper. The water purls above my knees and fondles my thighs almost arousing even as it chills me. From out of the everywhere, I think of Virginia Woolf drowning herself.

How was she able to do it?

Oh, yes, enough heavy stones in her pocket and an even

heavier weight on her heart. And then a lowering into an indifferent embrace.

I could do it, I tell myself, if I put my mind to it.

Is not suicide nothing more than another task?

I could do it.

If my life demanded it.

If my Lucas does not return.

I am standing in the deepest swing of the current—at my waist—when I intuit that I am being watched. On the bank where I had sat minutes earlier, I see Perry Ellis and Mr. Bonnard. The latter is eye balling me as if I have taken leave of my senses.

"Hey, there," I say, waving.

He returns the wave and says, "Y'all good 'n fine this mornin', Miss DeGresse?" There is concern in his tone.

"I am, sir. I am."

Perry Ellis, in the dark swirl of his sightless moments, pipes in: "Fishin' for cats, Miss DeGresse?"

I laugh.

"Not with my bare hands, no way."

He grins.

Awash in small talk, we head back to the cabin. They have brought ice, and Mr. Bonnard a basket of first-growth tomatoes for which I am warmly appreciative since I have neglected my own plantings of them. We drink glasses of iced tea so sweet that a Yankee would choke on them.

Then the inevitable.

"Miss DeGresse, we have not located your brother. That ole swamp is bigger than uh body thinks, and Cat Bells, it done don't have an end nobody knows 'bout."

"Should not we form up a search party?" I say.

He shakes his head.

"Your brother, ma'am, he knows this here area. Not likely he's lost. The boy here, he tells me your brother maybe done jus' needs some time alone—y'all think that might could be?"

"Yes, I believe Perry Ellis could be correct. I shall try to be patient, but it is powerfully difficult."

"Ma'am, I done knowed it is. I done knowed it is."

Perry Ellis smiles crookedly at me.

"I be prayin' harder. Prayin' till I breaks out in a sweat."

"Do not harm yourself greatly," I say, and I smile at him through an eddy of threatening tears, and I thank the two of them for their generosity and their humanity.

In the heat of the afternoon I sleep, and I dream that I was swallowed by a catfish as big as my cabin. Gracious goodness, has my mind gone all the way around the bend?

The moon rises full, saturated with silence and an indifferent whiteness in contrast to the raucous, darkly seeking trio that disturbs the path to my cabin. There is laughter. There are the hoots of the young. There is singing, but no song with which I am familiar.

It is a joyous, unsettling trinity: Cavatina, Perry Ellis, and Allegra.

Despite myself, I smile at their approach.

So alive they are. So alive.

I hope that my Lucas will join us, but I am doubtful.

Cavatina, as usual the loudest of the gang, barely has on clothes at all. She has looped the scarecrow's rope around the waist of Perry Ellis and is pulling him into my light as if he is her slave. The out-of-control smile on his face signals that he does not mind, not one bit.

Allegra brings up the rear. Cavatina points at her and exclaims,

"Look at this: I got her to ditch that fuckin' bathrobe."

It is true. Allegra is wearing a new pair of blue jeans and a white, knit top. She looks stunning. She smiles at me and waves, clutching her violin case to her stomach.

I invite them to sit. We have glasses of wine, and I relax and listen to their inane chatter; no one seems in the mood for a reading. Cavatina displays the cross and dagger carving Perry Ellis gave to her. It is evident that he is falling in love with her, that he wants her. Even in the eyes of the blind, one can see lust.

"Hey, guys, watch this."

Cavatina suddenly takes the dagger point and presses it against her wrist. Blood blossoms. Allegra frowns, in disapproval, I believe. Then Cavatina grabs one hand of Perry Ellis, and before he can protest, she does the same to his wrist.

"Gracious goodness," I whisper. I am horrified.

The mouth of Perry Ellis hangs open slackly. Cavatina kisses it with an audible smack.

"Here's the deal," she says. "This is our bond of blood—means we've hooked up." She brings the wounds together as if she is intent upon binding their wrists permanently. "There—blood is the life," she chortles, kissing Perry Ellis slap on one of his eyes. He blinks rapidly and giggles. He is smitten. I feel a vague unease. What can I do?

Seeming to ignore them, Allegra scoots her chair closer to mine and says, "Is your brother not coming tonight?"

I shrug. Death cannot find a foothold in her. I sense it.

"I have not seen him for several days. I trust that he is fine."

"I'm sure he is." She hesitates. I feel the inner breeze of her need to confide in me. I almost stop her. "He is a remarkable man," she says. "I've never met anyone like him."

She smiles into my face as if she wants me to understand something beyond her words.

Of course, I agree with her sentiments.

"I hope he is not lost," I say, much too aware of the ambiguity of my words.

Her eyes brighten, somehow too alert, too knowing.

"Not lost," she says. "He is waking."

I tell myself that I do not understand. I cannot find words to respond, and so I get up and stumble inside the cabin for more wine. When I return, Cavatina and Allegra are talking about someone named "Jenny," a friend of theirs who apparently serves as their taxi from Sweet River to my property. Pleased that my Lucas is no longer the topic of conversation, I offer that this Jenny is welcome to join us some night.

The evening settles ahead of my capacity to anticipate.

As if rays from the moon high in the western night cue her, Allegra removes her violin and notes that Max Bruch is one of her favorite composers. She wants to share the beauty of his music. But before she can bring bow to strings, she is interrupted by Cavatina who jokes about the full moon and werewolves, and Perry Ellis directs our attention to Resurrection Fern.

I gasp.

Our Lady of the Scarecrow is sporting a wax hand, five fingers plain as day, and the tip of each finger is a burning wick. Cavatina grins and shoves at Perry Ellis: "Good job, demon boy!"

Allegra's stare at the weird creation possesses a spectral cast.

Hand of Glory—the phrase surfaces in my thoughts from somewhere, and I experience a chill. Silence thickens. Marauder and Jacob, on the edge of our gathering, breathe soundlessly, but their ears, I believe, are pricked.

Allegra looks at me, her eyes glimmering with reassurance.

"Your Lucas is nearby. Don't doubt it."

She straightens in her chair and begins to play—the music is ravishing.

The moon and stars seem quietly closer than normal.

As the wine goes to my head, I sense that Allegra is right. My Lucas, off in the darkness passing, must be listening, having awakened to the mystical strains of life, a life with no further need of the Beast.

June 25

Not long after midnight I woke, suddenly aware of weird noises. The wine gurgling in my head, I rolled off the cot where I had been catnapping. My trio of visitors was nowhere to be seen. My fire pit had burned low. My lantern had dimmed.

Those noises?

A forced, high-pitched laughter for one.

Then quavering notes of fear.

Poor Marauder stood at the border of light and darkness and—I swear this to be true—he was so frightened of something that he hooted like an owl. It was chilling to hear. And, Jacob, I could have sworn that he was growling. Growling!

I glanced out at Resurrection Fern, and I must have imagined this: issuing from her a grinding, muted scream as if she could not breathe—like the terrified voice of the woods. I had heard it before, especially those first nights I spent in the cabin alone.

I soothed the two animals; I ignored Resurrection Fern.

Had the Beast passed close by?

I stoked my fire and sat and thought.

I began to entertain a vision of Allegra as a vampire arisen from a grave she had conquered to seek out a man who could not live so that she might feed upon him and live more livingly.

Yes, it was a silly notion.

I thought of my family: the House of DeGresse—how we had fallen from—or was it into?—the pages of Poe.

A fresh round of laughter drew me through the darkness to the bank of the pond where a small fire burned, illuminating two almost naked figures: Cavatina and Perry Ellis. Clad only in underpants, they seemed unreal, the white of the garments too luminous in the firelight.

As Perry Ellis danced and grinned and clapped his hands, Cavatina shrieked, her laughter out of control. At moments, she yanked on the rope noosed around his neck. Profanities peppered her guffawing.

I pitied Perry Ellis, though I am not sure why.

Had I served him up to damnation, to the creature that is Cavatina, one not just immoral but amoral? Oh, Perry Ellis, are you truly a demon boy? Where is your Jesus now?

I turned away in disgust and groped towards the trailer of my Lucas. One light, a low, bronzed light, burned within it. Were they inside—Allegra and my Lucas? I do not know how long I stood there, an icon of waiting in the night air, before something astonishing occurred.

The voice of my Lucas rising in the hovering darkness, a ghostly, magnificent sound that filled the woods; it was an auditory apparition of memory, echoing through the treetops and sweeping past me indifferently, causing itself to be heard yet not fully understood. It was an aria, I believe, a snatch of one, offered timidly and uncertainly at first, before gaining its legs and acquiring volume. It was my Lucas, the tenor of such promise, living in song once again, releasing passion and fire and beauty. Such a voice does not originate in one's body, but rather it is birthed in the spirit.

The voice was its own eros—a mystery moving beyond clues.

So overjoyed was I to hear my Lucas sing again that I fell to my knees and thanked the haunted ground beneath me for the arrival of Allegra, the one who did not die so that the fates could allow her to bring another being back to life.

June 26

"Jessica Love, I'm here."

Not fully awake, I glance up from my coffee. The warm, dry air of the morning shoves its way into my cabin. I hear birds. I hear Marauder panting excitedly, and, more in the distance, a snickering bray from Jacob.

My Lucas, his hair wet as if slicked down with dew, braces himself in the doorway. Though his eyes are red and preternaturally alert as if he has not slept, he smiles, animating his face almost comically.

Were someone watching us, the scene could be read as melodramatic: I push away from the table, knocking my chair over, and, an expression of gladness throttled high in my chest, I run to him; he squeezes life, not *out* of me, but *in* to me. He lifts me off the floor—I scream delightedly—and he swings my body to and fro.

We speak in hushed, incoherent words. We speak rapidly.

Both of us are crying.

We stagger to the table, and when the foam of elation has subsided, we sit and stare and smile into each other's face as if thirsty for the moments of exchange, and then we talk.

Later, I will only recall snatches of our conversation.

"I heard you singing," I say. "It was indescribable. It was something I had been longing for—I could hardly believe my ears."

"Yes," he says. "I finally have reason to sing. I have songs."

"What happened?" I ask, but, of course, as a woman, I know.

"Jessica Love," he says, clutching at my wrists, "I'm unearthing myself. I won't stay buried."

"It was Allegra, was it not?"

"Yes, my God, yes—yes, yes, yes. She brought me back to life."

I listen. Suddenly I am so many pieces of flotsam and jetsam in a flooding body of water. I swirl. I let the flow of his words carry me downstream, destination unknown.

I say little, voice some concern about the differences in their ages and about how they have only been in each other's company for a few days. I bring up the psychological trauma she has experienced and how she is still recovering.

"No one," he says, "understands trauma more than I do. Iraq was my journey into that realm, my Inferno. I understand who Allegra is. Together the two of us know about life and death in ways most everybody else can't possibly know."

He is right. I confess to myself that he is right.

He declares that he is going to clean up the clutter in his life and move on.

"What about the Beast?" I ask. "What about the ghost of our father?"

He looks away. He turns in his chair and gazes out through the door into the sun-splashed woods. When he twists back to face me, he taps his temple and says, "The Beast is up here." And then he presses his fingers against his heart. "Our father is in here. That's how I see it now—now that I can live again."

He has a request: tomorrow evening we—Allegra, he, Cavatina, Perry Ellis, and I—have a nice dinner here in the cabin. A celebration. He wants me to read to them after dinner. I say that I shall be pleased to do so.

For the remainder of the day, he, with the assistance of the other members of the foursome, attacks his trailer and, in trip after trip, hauls away the physical mess of his life in the bed of his pickup. I am hurt somewhat that they do not ask me to help.

They are young; I am not.

There are in love with life, playing in its arena; I am merely a spectator.

June 27

As I stroll listlessly on the bordering path between my property. and the Nahollo Swamp, I lose myself in speculation. The morning air is steamy; accordingly, Marauder and Jacob, wiser than I, have held back. I have draped a cold, wet towel around my neck like a friendly boa constrictor.

My Lucas is a man deeply in love, but not simply in love with a woman, with Allegra. No, he has fallen into an uncommon love for living, a love that had been tied up in his capacity to sing—song is his being. That being has now been released. No one lacking an affection for living can possibly give voice the way he can. It is as if singing has put him back in touch with the earthly beauty and anguish of living. He has opened his eyes and opened his heart.

All because, I must admit, of another woman.

Allegra.

In her, my Lucas has found a woman from the yesterday of beyond. With her, he can start anew again and again. In her, he has discovered a place in which to begin living.

A vague, ironic notion sweeps through me: if Cavatina had not wandered out of the darkness into my world weeks ago, none of this would have occurred. And now, Perry Ellis, too, has been gifted—with love or, more certainly, lust, and although I am troubled by his relationship with Cavatina, who am I to judge it?

I am the keeper of those who fall.

No, I am *not* a keeper. My role in life seems more to be a voyeur.

Gracious goodness. So it is.

Mid-morning, my Lucas takes me grocery shopping. All the way to Sweet River and back, he chirps about Allegra, about what she has done for him, and about his plans for the future—*their* plans for the future.

I try as hard as I can to be happy for him.

And at one point he says to me: "You gone be fine, Jessica Love?"

His question surprises the breath out of me. I force some words in the strongest tone I can muster: "I shall be. I truly shall be."

Yet, I am uncertain.

When we return, my Lucas shows me his now spotless trailer. Seeing that he has restored order to his living space, I say, "It looks so very nice." I reach for his neck. "I am so happy for you, sweetheart."

"I need that. I need for you to understand this change in my life. It's sudden—I know. But it's real."

My words barely audible, I say, "I do understand."

He hugs me firmly, and I float back to my cabin. I feel everything. I feel nothing.

Thankfully, cooking for our big supper erases the incoherent chalkings of my thoughts.

As evening approaches, I put on a dress. My face wades into my mirror. I have to work at looking presentable. What flits through my mind are winging thoughts: I wish I could be as attractive as Cavatina and Allegra and I wish I could be a young woman again. My mirror pushes an older woman's countenance out from the glass, gently reminding me not to abandon my reflection, for it holds a larger truth.

Twilight is bewitching. A dark ruffle of stray clouds becomes threadbare as a full moon rises, grips the woods and pours light through the thick, warm air. My eating table is a touch romantic: a chorus of candles and a decorative bowl filled with cuttings of nandina, astilbe, and Christmas fern. My guests begin to arrive—all four are dressed up. Everyone is quite handsome, quite lovely. Everyone hugs, everyone smiles, and everyone seems to need to talk at the same time. I am dizzied.

We sit down to a mid-summer feast: fried chicken, baked beans, potato salad, tomatoes, okra, and yellow squash. Allegra has brought a banana cream pie—a favorite of my Lucas. Perry Ellis offers a ripe, Charleston Gray watermelon to our fare. We have iced tea and wine to drink.

I glance around. The candlelight bronzes us. Quite suddenly, I find myself choking back tears: "You are my Good Faces," I say. "Thank you all for coming. Please know that I love you all dearly. I do."

Allegra pats my wrist.

"We love you, too."

"Damn straight," adds Cavatina.

"Jesus loves y'all—doncha forget dat."

We laugh nervously, sincerely, at Perry Ellis.

My Lucas, prompted by something beyond words, I believe, stands up. Our scene falls into silence. We lean into his self-consciousness, and this is what he says:

"I have learned … that life is in the right—a body's not really living if he doesn't have folks he loves and who love him."

We murmur agreement.

My Lucas smiles at me, and the affection it carries gusts through me. I am solemnly joyful. I recover and surprise Perry Ellis by asking him to say grace.

We eat with an almost sacred resolution; it is as if we are sharing a last supper.

When we gather in reverie near the fire pit after dessert, we are as full as ticks. Even Marauder and Jacob have participated in our bounty; Resurrection Fern has donned a new, black cape, tricked out with sparkling, albeit cheap, sequins. She is silent. She abides.

Cavatina and Perry Ellis, Allegra and my Lucas snuggle in spaces they have created, rewarded, it seems, for waiting for what wanted to come.

And then my announcement: "I feel like reading Whitman."

There is a tittering of approval and bemused applause.

When I have taken enough glittery swallows of wine, I begin to adore the sound of my voice. Whitman sings through my every pore: "O Captain! my Captain!"—and I feel that great star droop and hear hidden birds warbling, and I have the taste of Whitman's genius on my tongue.

Whitman sings on.

I serve only to amplify. And I, too, praise the fathomless universe.

Endlessly rocking. Endlessly rocking.

With love, with love.

The aria sinking.

I read, but I do not know the difference between demon and bird.

The night whispers me.

When my Lucas, minutes and minutes later, lifts the book from my hands, he asks if I would like to hear him sing. I nod. He stands at the center of our circle—a new circle, freshly drawn—and the voice of my Lucas sweeps me out of my body. My beloved brother releases into the magic of our tiny community the grand melodies of Puccini.

They are astonishingly beautiful.

Oh, solitary me listening.

And the time slips away.

The two couples eventually bleed off through the mystical veins of the moment.

My heart stops.

But I force it to beat again.

I am myself alone.

Yet, company arrives—for I imagine our Whitman there with me in a free flight into the wordless. We talk softly about the themes we love best: night, sleep, death, and the stars.

June 28

L ove is space being used without space being taken.
What can be said then about taking up space without using it?

The opposite of love is not hate—it is inertia.

This is what happens when I mix three glasses of wine with the poetry of Whitman: my thoughts clog with sludgy banality.

I sleep in. I ignore the dirty dishes.

To clear my head, I walk, late morning, beyond the pond; I can feel the primordial heat of Nahollo Swamp. The back entrance to Cat Bells seems to brood. I shall not enter it, though the cool mass of darkness within appeals to me—if I stare into it, will it return the stare and eventually invite me over the threshold?

I wander along, my eyes drawn to the ground—I am wary wise regarding snakes, and because I have been looking down, I have lost track of Marauder and Jacob. But when I hear barking, I glance up in time to see someone on a dirt bike swerve and then crash.

"Goodness," I murmur and hasten to the scene.

It is a young man. Early twenties, I would guess. I lean down over him and the twisted snarl of his bike. After we establish that he is not seriously injured, he says that his name is "Tevis." He seems quite different from the typical run of dirt bikers along this trail who sport colorful helmets and tight, colorful outfits that remind me of circus performers.

He looks bohemian. He wears a brimless cap and a long-sleeved, dark shirt, dark trousers, and tall boots. His black, slightly curled hair, almost touching his shoulders, resembles

the silken feathers of a crow. His face startles me, for he possesses something akin to feminine features—lips heart-shaped
like a young woman's, a flawless, aquiline nose, a black bridge
of eyebrows and eyes set abnormally far apart that hold sadness and wonder—lovely, lovely eyes, black rimmed as if he has
applied mascara. He is around six feet tall; his hands and fingers are long and girlishly smooth.

I blink away the otherworldly effect of him.

Although he is basically unhurt, he seems disoriented. From
a backpack, he retrieves a plastic bottle of water and drinks
long. He explains himself. He is looking for an entrance to Cat
Bells and asks about the pond. He does not realize that it is on
my property. His tone is apologetic.

"I didn't know I was trespassing."

"We are all trespassers on this earth," I say.

I tell him little about myself.

In contrast, he is open about himself. He has been a stu-
dent at Mantis College in Sweet River studying graphic design
before switching to fine arts—drawing and painting are his
passions. His voice is soft, arresting. And then our conversation
shifts and something stirs within me.

"I like the wilderness," he says. "I'm a fan of Thoreau—I can
see myself living the pages of *Walden*."

I hesitate. I feel the onslaught of an old belonging.

"Thoreau struggled some with his experiment," I say.

"So you've read *Walden*?"

I do not want to leave. I need to talk. And so I do. About having been a teacher. About my interest in American literature.
About my cabin. About my desire to heal myself: solitude and
reading. I do not mention my Lucas or the others.

His beautiful eyes widen.

"The poetry of Whitman," he says, "often spurs my
emotions."

"Yes. I feel the same way."

"Do you think Thoreau and Whitman ever met? Wouldn't
that have been an interesting pair? Can you imagine them
together?"

I nod.

"They did, in fact, meet. In 1856." I pause to study his expression, and in it I read that he truly wants me to continue. I begin talking as if I am very hungry to teach again. I mention all that I know about Thoreau's view of Whitman and vice versa. I smile into a memory of something Thoreau wrote to a friend about Whitman's poetry:

"It is as if the beasts spoke."

Why did I specifically recall that line?

Tevis laughs.

"Then, he didn't like Whitman's work?"

"Oh, I think, for the most part, he did. I think he rather admired the man, too. There was apparently a mutual liking, a mutual respect, I believe."

"What about Emerson and Whitman?"

"Well, of course, Whitman sought Emerson's approval, and he received it."

How long did the young man and I talk? I am not certain.

We conversed at least until he became aware that he needed to return to Sweet River.

"You are welcome on my property," I said.

He smiled.

"I'd like to return. I like exploring the swamp and these woods. I like caves. Thanks for sharing what you know about Thoreau and Whitman." Then he interrupted the rhythm of his speech. "I'm glad I wrecked."

June 29

Morning seems a good time to read Thoreau's *Journal*. I take notes assiduously as I engage the lines, aware of his youthful perception and wisdom as I move from entry to entry. I work as if I am preparing a lesson for class. Where are my students? I suddenly miss them. I imagine the face of Tevis and wonder whether he will return.

Perry Ellis drags in. He carries his Bible comfortingly, the way a child does a favorite toy—a teddy bear or a rag doll—for companionship no human can provide. He is moping. When he drops his chin onto my table, I cannot suppress a chuckle.

"Down in the dumps, Perry Ellis?"

He sighs.

I fix him a cup of coffee. I return to Thoreau.

My strategy succeeds. My young friend opens up with musings about my Lucas and Allegra, about how he thinks they may live together in the trailer or that they may run off together, get shet of Alabama. He sounds more confused than troubled.

I listen. I stiffen before I control myself and speak.

"They are free to choose, I assume. My only concern is their happiness."

Perry Ellis frowns.

"Dey in love?"

"I believe so."

"Allegra, she nice."

I allow a silence to fill the spaces between us.

"Do you think she is a good person? She certainly seems to be."

He nods. Then I realize that it is not Allegra and my Lucas

weighing heavily in his thoughts.

"What am I gone do?" he groans.

Once again, a chuckle escapes my attempt to curtail it. I give him a nudge. I present myself as his confessor. He exhales into a narrative of being conflicted—naturally, at the center of his bewilderment is Cavatina.

"I been hearin' voices 'bout her."

He claims that he is besieged by demons urging him on in his desire for Cavatina and by the fatherly intoning of God spelling out all that is sinful about his lustful ways. I listen until I grow impatient.

"Good gracious, Perry Ellis, this is just about *sex*—every person on this good planet Earth experiences difficulties in these matters." I shake my head. "Did I not warn you about Cavatina?"

"She make my heart hurt."

"Of course she does." I pat his Bible. I press closer to him. "Does not your scripture here claim that this too shall pass?"

"Yes, ma'am."

But his pulings continue.

My exasperation is fueled.

"What if you were my age, Perry Ellis?"

The moment begins to unravel.

He looks puzzled. He thinks I am angry with him. Truth is, I suppose I am. Words slip into a greasy funnel.

"What about me?" I say, raising my voice.

My emotions torch.

"What about what *I* need?"

I rant into the morning heat.

I cannot stop myself.

"What about me? What about *me*?" I scream. I slap the table surface, and the sound is that of a report from a rifle.

Surprised, shaken by my outburst, Perry Ellis steals hurriedly into the day.

In the emptiness of my cabin, I press my face into my hands. After a few minutes, I fear that when I pull away, my face will not be a face at all, only a blank, featureless mask of flesh.

June 30

I want to get to a place beyond anger and fear and self-pity.

July 1

A new month.
I pledge a new Jessica Lovelia DeGresse.

I stay in my cabin all day and read Dickinson: "I lived on Dread—"

How significantly *dread* rhymes with *bread*.

I write to Aunt Julia, and I tell her that mother should spend her final days wherever she would like. She has a right to return to this property if she so chooses. What I do not say haunts the empty spaces of the letter.

When darkness falls, I light candles and have an intense rendezvous with familiar shadows.

But I do not know who I am or where I have hidden my life.

July 2

I was cheered, mid-morning, on my path up by Cat Bells, for Tevis, wearing coveralls like an auto mechanic, crawled free of the small opening to the cave system just as I was passing. His smile, warm and bright, complemented his stunning eyes. He was quick to greet me as he brushed dust from his sleeves. Then he shook his head and glanced back at the round darkness of the entrance.

"That place is incredible."

"I find it scary," I said.

Something in his effeminate beauty almost caused me to blush.

He slithered his hand through the air.

"Amazing the way it snakes around and without warning leads you up to a deep shaft. I found at least one that didn't seem to have a bottom when I dropped a good-sized rock down it. And the blackness is so thick that my flashlight is barely of any use."

"Please be careful." I hesitated. My face must have reddened even as we talked. "To me, it seems so very strange. Like the Underworld of mythology."

He chuckled and shook his head again, and we chatted a bit more as I composed myself. He asked whether he might, before the summer ended, pitch a tent and camp out by my pond—"To imitate Thoreau," he said. I told him that would be fine. Later, I felt that I should not have agreed quite so readily.

Then he said, "Oh, hey—do you know a woman who's called, 'Sister Speakes'?"

I smiled knowingly.

"Everyone in the vicinity of Nahollo Swamp does. She is the elderly fortune teller and herbalist. She lives in a hovel about a half a mile back to the west."

"I've heard she's a healer, too. A friend of mine said she is. Any truth to the rumors about her?"

Because he seemed serious beyond curiosity, I told him most of what I knew about Opal Speakes, the so-called swamp doctor who could, allegedly, read the future, and about how the aged crone lived by herself, a white woman who, for the most part, served black customers and likely sold nonsense and bogus cures.

What I did not tell him was that back in April, when my Lucas began to teeter on the brink of something that terrified me, I played with the notion of paying the old woman a visit: what might she offer for a man slipping into madness with the vengeful ghost of his father and the specter of an imaginary "Beast" haunting him?

At the last minute, I had thought better of it.

Tevis listened attentively.

"So," he said, "you've seen this woman? You know what she looks like?"

I nodded.

"She resembles a cedar knee only more wrinkled and grayer. An ancient, bent-over, gipsy-like woman who knows that ole swamp inside and out."

He smiled at my imagery.

"Would love to meet her."

I returned the smile.

"Best watch it—she might put a hex on you."

"Could she do that?"

I shrugged.

"Sister Speakes—to her followers, at least—has the power to make a cottonmouth moccasin as eloquent as Shakespeare."

We left each other smiling as the morning heat rose beneath our feet.

It is later now, in the cabin, out of the fierce sun, a sun of wolves hunting the east Alabama landscape. I have new company.

"You good to go with Allegra and Lucas, you know, shackin' up?"

Cavatina, her face vibrant with a sheen of sweat, drinks her iced tea as she waits for me to respond. It is nearing noon, and we have spent a good deal of time touring my property, talking about plants, insects, animals, and reptiles. Possessing at least a superficial interest, Cavatina has listened, I assume, to much I have said. Whether she retains the information is hard to say. She seems especially enamored of my woodland plantings near the cabin—the ferns, wild ginger, and creeping jenny.

"If they want to do that, I have no objections. I want only good things for my Lucas … and for Allegra, too, of course."

"You don't hate my sister for takin' him away? I mean, shit, I know you really have this strange thing for him?"

"Strange thing?"

My throat starts to burn.

"Oh, hell, you know what I mean. Come on. I ain't blind."

"I do not have a 'strange thing'—whatever that may be—for my Lucas. I have a perfectly warm and sisterly love for him."

But I am a poor liar. I am suddenly tired, and my heart feels heavy in my chest, and I do not want to talk about my Lucas. The good feelings from having talked with Tevis earlier have evaporated.

Cavatina shrugs.

"Me, I think they should just get the fuck out of Alabama. Out of the whole God damn South, you know. Go some other place. They need that—doncha think?"

"Perhaps."

But I would not want to go on living if my Lucas went away.

Cavatina tells me that he has totally changed her sister's life. Healed it. She tells me that my Lucas is exactly what Allegra needs.

My mind sluggishly shifts gears.

I do not believe that Cavatina has met Tevis, and I am not eager for her to do so. My thoughts on the matter are vague, inchoate.

I ask about her mother. I ask again what her mother thinks of Allegra and my Lucas, their relationship, their closeness.

Cavatina merely laughs and informs me that her mother has taken off to Ft. Myers, Florida, for five or six weeks to be with her "drinkin' buddies" and to kill off their remaining brain cells. I am appalled.

"Who is taking care of you?" I ask.

She snickers smugly.

"Me, myself, and I," she says and winks.

Unwisely, I suppose, I express my concern for Perry Ellis and for her effect upon the young man. Much as I expected, she dismisses it as a problem.

"Shit, we're just havin' fun. I like him."

"But he does not seem able to handle his ... his affection for you."

"All guys think with their dicks. Perry Ellis is no fuckin' different from nobody else."

I chide myself for wasting my breath. I want to plead with her not to hurt him or not to provoke him to hurt himself, but our conversation thuds to a conclusion. Minutes later, breaking the oppressive silence, a stranger appears at the door.

"Oh, hey," says Cavatina, "this here's Jenny Ballou, a good friend. I call her 'Creepy Jenny,' you know, after the plant."

The woman hesitating in the doorway is very thin with graying hair combed mannishly in a sweep across her head. She has a poor complexion, bad teeth of which she is self-conscious, and eyes that are gray and dying though friendly. She wears a long-sleeved work shirt, blue jeans, and boots.

We have a brief exchange, and I get a peculiar feeling when the woman looks at Cavatina and even more so when at one point she says, with her eyes cutting towards her, "I think the whole world of this girl here. I'd do anything for her."

Cavatina hugs her and then to me says, "You still OK with Jenny comin' some night when you're readin'?"

"Of course," I say.

July 3

"Allegra, she loves Cat Bells. I think she could live there." My Lucas sits with his fingers curled around a glass of iced tea. His face is bright and shining with love for the new woman in his life, and while I am pleased for him, I cannot, as always, be elated. Places deep inside me ache. Places closer to the surface burn with brush fires of jealousy.

"You are fortunate," I say, "to find someone who likes this area—some folks see it as being depressing. They cannot fit it into their hearts."

My Lucas is only barely listening.

"Allegra, she even loves the swamp. Can you fathom that?"

"Well, it has beautiful spots in it, but, mostly, it feels like a piece of our planet where nobody human belongs."

My Lucas looks away. He stares into the warm shadows of my abode and wherever he has taken himself, no one else can follow. He leaves neither tracks nor traces. After a few moments, he smiles his way back.

"*I* belong with Allegra," he says.

His tone is melodramatic; it grates on me. Then, under his breath, he repeats his words, and I feel a stab. Am I bleeding within? Or am I just being foolish, imagining pain that, for some reason, I *need* to feel?

"Does *she* belong with *you*?"

He nods emphatically as he pushes away from the table, handsome, strong, no ghost of his once-upon-a-time obsessions haunting him. He has been exorcized, or so it seems.

"She told me she does. She told me that she'll be with me always. Just like that. She said, 'Lucas, I'll be with you always.'"

He swallows back a rush of emotion, an invisible something pouring through him, a something he needs and must trust. Of course, I have no genuine response, only my faith in faithlessness. I feel an icy scrim upon my heart.

I tell him that I plan to read tonight if anyone is interested. Then I hug him, pressing myself into his warmth, hoping that when he is gone I shall hear half the gladness that sings throughout his body.

I watch him leave.

… *always, always, always.*

Such a word keeps us alive, preventing us from surrendering to the forces of dead realities.

When evening steals upon the woods, I feel terribly alone.

I cannot explain it. The dark lyrics of my life are far more complex and unreadable than my narratives. I prepare for what wants to come. Resurrection Fern looks as old as I feel; mosquitoes swarm about her hideous grin. Marauder, panting like a small engine, plops down by the fire pit. I notice that Jacob stands nearby, like a sentinel; he swishes his tail, one gleaming eye catching the arrival of an indifferent gloaming.

My guests appear, drifting in rather like fog. They create a gathering node of soft laughter and speech. There is evident though muted elation in their being here—I feel a surge of thankfulness. Good Faces.

Tonight we shall sacrifice the Beast of Solitude.

I notice right away, of course, that Cavatina is with Jenny. Allegra clutches lovingly at my Lucas. Her eyes see only him and whatever lurks in the nimbus of his presence.

Not tactfully I say to Cavatina, "Where is Perry Ellis?"

She chuckles in her chest.

"Off bein' a sorry ass." Then more benign chuckles. "I brought Creepy Jenny instead. She's my gal pal."

Jenny offers half a smile, then draws a curtain on her bad teeth with her hand. Her eyes flash embarrassment as they meet mine and my welcome. Allegra floats over and hugs my neck, whispering, "I need to ask a favor of you."

I nod, confused, not certain that I have heard her precisely.

She returns to be by the side of my Lucas who smiles the

neutral smile of a good brother and salutes me with three
fingers.

I offer wine.

And I toast surprise: a tall stranger, a beauty in his eyes not
even Keats could describe, a gentle shyness in his manner that
lives between the lines of a medieval ballad.

I welcome Tevis, who says he is camping out by the pond,
and I assure him that he is not trespassing. Then introductions
all around and small talk is exchanged as I hunt up another
chair, more wine, another glass. When I return, I overhear my
Lucas, Allegra, and Tevis chatting about Cat Bells. Cavatina is
kissing Jenny on the ear just the way she has kissed Perry Ellis.

I feel left out.

I announce that I shall read from *The Journal* of Thoreau. I
snare the appreciative twinkle in the eyes of Tevis. Suddenly
I am very glad that he is here. We settle into the rhythms of
Thoreau's aphoristic prose. We are haloed by the fumes of wine
and the steamy reek of boiled peanuts that my Lucas purchased
in Sweet River. Later, there is marijuana. I am the only one who
does not engage it.

I release myself to get high on Thoreau.

My voice catches the wave of relentless words.

I must confess there is nothing so strange to me as my own body.

...

*I am like a feather floating in the atmosphere; on every side is depth
unfathomable.*

...

*There must be some narrowness in the soul that compels one to
have secrets.*

...

Our doubts are so musical that they persuade themselves.

I read until my listeners are beyond listening, and I am
beyond reading. I offer a final morsel of Thoreau: "See what a
life the gods have given us, set round with pain and pleasure. It
is too strange for sorrow; it is too strange for joy."

I bow to the applause of my traveling gods. I say goodnight
and add that they are welcome to stay and embrace the reverie
of night and stars and the shadow of the Beast. They laugh as

softly as a breeze through the leaves high in a poplar tree.

Tired in my bones, I go to bed, and I hear them, faintly, talking, laughing, even singing a bit—and I am that child again who will fall asleep to the reassuring sounds of adults conversing. I breathe in the irony of the moment.

… too strange for sorrow; … too strange for joy.

July 4

Fully awake, I lie in my bed and recall that Allegra wants to ask a favor of me. What could it be? There was not a good opportunity for us to talk at my reading last night, and so now I scratch at my curiosity, realizing that I do not know Allegra. I should make more of an effort to. And yet—can one ever be close to a woman who will not die and who loves the man you love?

I rise. Daylight is burning. And because it is our national holiday, I pole our father's American flag at the front of my cabin just as was his yearly practice. I would not call myself a super patriot, but I am thankful that I live in this country, and I believe that our flag is the most beautiful on the planet. I glance around. If the ghost of our father lurks, I assume that he is pleased to see what I have done. When I glimpse the outline of Resurrection Fern, I can imagine that she has placed her hand over her heart in due respect.

Back in my kitchen, I find myself thinking of Tevis.

No ghost. A real, young man. Lovely, gracious, intelligent, sensitive.

I suddenly have an idea, excitement purls through me. I bake up a batch of biscuits, spoon out dollops of scuppernong grape jelly on a plate and head for the pond. I am thrilled to see that he is awake, sitting by his bright orange dome of a tent. He is sketching something, his eyes volleying from his drawing pad to the sun-glistened surface of the pond and back.

I compose myself as I approach.

"Are you enjoying playing at being Thoreau?"

His face bursts into a smile when he recognizes me.

"How did he survive without bug spray?" he says.

We laugh together. I sit with him, and he gratefully accepts my offering of biscuits and jelly. He shares with me his pencil sketch of the pond and of three or four soft-shelled turtles getting an early jump on their daily basking.

"It is remarkably good," I murmur.

He tears out the sheet and gives it to me in exchange for the biscuits. It is a good moment. I feel twenty-five years younger, but then I rein in myself, and I am struck deeply by something Tevis says about his artistic skill:

"At a certain point—if I submit to the process—I discover that it's not a matter of my looking at things and trying to capture them but rather that things are looking at me, and that they've entered the drawing even before I put pencil to the paper."

"That sounds almost mystical."

We talk further. I sense that he has been galvanized by this setting. He seems to belong here. Invariably, of course, we begin to talk about *Walden*. I follow the labyrinth of our exchange. Along the way, however, something extraordinary occurs: I hear his words, and I experience a *frisson*—I cannot readily dismiss what I am hearing.

"When I'm on your property," he says, "or when I'm in Cat Bells or over in Nahollo Swamp, I think about Thoreau's line: 'The wildest scenes had become accountably familiar.'" Our eyes meet, and he continues. "I know what he means. There's something spiritual as well as savage out here. Something familiar. Don't you feel it?"

I swallow back the approach of genuine fear.

"I try *not* to."

Silken threads of silence connect us until he continues.

"I've encountered something strange," he says, "something very strange."

"Sister Speakes?"

My attempt to be deflective raises a smile, but I can see that Tevis is deadly serious—that he needs to confide.

"No," he says. "Nothing human."

What he goes on to tell me makes my heart race because it touches upon a belief in a "subtle reality," in what might be termed the supra-sensible, a realm permeating an intermediate space between physical and mental reality. He describes hearing the rush and crash of a very large creature; he describes having heard eerie sounds. He spews it all out, but along the way I force myself to stop listening.

At the end of his confession, he says the expected: "You think I'm crazy?"

I shake my head.

"I think you have been bitten—by the darkness, the mystery of things."

But I know that I must be fair, and so I share my narrative of the Beast, of what my Lucas had been engaged in before the arrival of Allegra. Tevis listens, seemingly, with every cell of his body.

At the completion of my account, we have nothing substantial to say. It seems that one either embraces mystery or rejects it totally. Closer because of the agnostic stance we adhere to, we part company.

But I sense something uncompanionable in the air.

The summer has long shadows, longer than I have anticipated.

That evening, I find that Tevis has folded up his tent and left the pond. He alluded to having an ailing friend in Sweet River he needed to visit. My Lucas, Allegra, Cavatina, and Jenny are going to the fireworks display there. They ask me to join them, but, of course, I decline.

I sit by my fire pit.

I admire the drawing Tevis gave me.

But then I begin to think of Allegra.

Something shouts in my ear: "Do it!"

In Poe's "The Imp of the Perverse," he never tells us who the "Imp" is. You must accept it as one of the insoluble mysteries of the soul. Poe wonders why Nature tempts us with such a voice, why we must *act for the reason that we should not.*

As I sit and think, shadows prevail upon me. I ponder my life, and as I stare into the flames I am irresistibly drawn to indulge a longing, and yet the most curious thing is that I do not know what, precisely, I long to do.

Only that it is destructive.

I, too, am becoming a victim of the Imp of the Perverse.

July 5

This morning I see Cavatina and Perry Ellis holding hands and wading in Deep Kill Creek. Perry Ellis is such a fool. Cavatina is so wicked. That new rope is looped around the neck of the young captive. The scene angers me; I would like to hang both of them. I would like to take my double-bladed hatchet to them. I sit on the bank and swat at gnats and watch them until Cavatina notices me, waves and gestures that I join them on a sandbar where raccoon tracks are evident.

A small, yet elegant, dark wood carving rests on the sand.

"Look't what my demon boy made with his knife—it's a gift, and I just love the shit out of it."

I hold it and examine it: a crazy-faced, naked-breasted woman stands atop a creature that is part bear and part man; the implication, I suppose, is that the woman controls the beast beneath her. Then, with a closer perusal, I detect that the face of the bear-man is clearly that of Perry Ellis. The woman could well be Cavatina.

"How appropriate," I say, my voice dripping with sarcasm.

Perry Ellis acts sheepish and Cavatina laughs her vile laugh. I think she may be on drugs of some kind, for she is manic, her eyes red and dead wild. I leave when she makes a salacious remark about Tevis, not one I choose to repeat.

Back at my cabin, I worry all day that Cavatina will steal Tevis from me (his friendship) just as Allegra stole my Lucas from me. I wish that these McKenna girls had never slithered their way into my Eden. Why am I not able to exile them forever?

Heat increases its grip on the woods.

I sleep on and off until evening. Allegra haunts my thoughts.

By candlelight I confess to Resurrection Fern that I want to help Allegra free the death that has been imprisoned within her. Am I selfish or selfless? Is this motiveless malignity? Am I plotting an exercise of humanity or of murder?

Prudently, Resurrection Fern remains silent.

I stoke my fire pit.

I receive no guests except my essential self.

I gaze into the flames—and a book title seizes my thoughts. "My Heart Laid Bare."

Of course, it is Poe. I recall what he wrote regarding the possibility that someone could write that book of endless self-denigration: "No man dare write it. No man ever will dare write it. No man could write it, even if he dared. The paper would shrivel and blaze at every touch of the fiery pen."

I resolve to prove Poe wrong.

"My Heart Laid Bare" shall become the title of my journal. Gentle Reader, you are witness to my cunningly insane revisioning of these summer days, of my dark sentencing by the fates.

I breathe morbid air.

I think poisonous thoughts.

July 6

Isteal away to the dairy section, but cannot elude Allegra. She has me in a dead reckoning, determined, it appears, to siphon off my patience and request something I doubt that I can give.

There is no place to hide in Wal-Mart. We are on a late morning shopping trip and my Lucas has wandered off to the automotive area or perhaps to hunting and fishing supplies. On our drive into Sweet River, I was almost sickened by how happy Allegra and my Lucas are. They sang and traded little displays of affection. I held my breath and stared at the bleakness of the passing landscape.

Before I left the cabin, I saw Perry Ellis and Cavatina riding bareback on Jacob. Marauder, silly-headed mutt that he is, trailed along behind them. They were laughing and hooting, filled with so much sexual energy that it should have been illegal. But I tell myself that I do not care.

Allegra looms at my right ear.

"Help me to know Lucas better—to know his world."

I cringe.

"I do not understand what you mean."

She is trembling. She whispers, "The swamp, Teach me about it the way you've been teaching Cavatina about the woods. I have to know what has always drawn Lucas to it—the swamp at night. And the Beast."

Despite the air conditioning running full blast, I can feel my upper lip starting to sweat. Allegra is unnerving. I would love to shed her, but I cannot.

"Have you not asked him yourself?"

"No. I couldn't do that. Besides, I want another woman as my guide."

My discomfort swells. My voice is cold.

"This does not sound like a good idea. I am sorry."

"Please." She grasps my arm. I can feel her warm blood pumping. There is something primitive in her presence, something of dark survival. "Please think about it. We could spend an evening exploring."

Exploring?

I am deeply puzzled. I am put off.

I shake my head.

"I cannot see how I can possibly help you."

"Please," she exclaims. "Please."

Returning home there is more singing, more displays of affection. The beautiful voice of my Lucas plucks at my heart. To hear him sing approaches being a mystical experience. I close my eyes. I am in the company of Orpheus and Eurydice. But shadows are filling my mind, things demonic to the faithful.

Why am I suddenly so fearful?

We leave most of the groceries at the trailer they now share. I part company with the lovebirds and carry my one small bag of necessities back to my cabin. I say hello to Resurrection Fern. She looks wilted.

And then I hear something.

At first, I do not recognize it.

Groaning?

I stop outside the cabin.

Someone is inside. I freeze. Am I being robbed?

The groans shade off into moans—grunts of pleasure, I believe. More than one person is violating my property.

I glance around for my watchdog. He is absent.

I take a deep breath. I march inside.

The shadows tumble and thrum, and at first I cannot grasp what I am witnessing: foreign movement, heightened, physical noises.

Then I see. Then I know.

On my cot, Perry Ellis and Cavatina appear to be wrestling; both are naked. I glimpse a sheen of sweat on the back of Perry

Ellis as he pumps and thrusts his body against and into the shimmering whiteness of Cavatina. He resembles an engine of some kind, the repetitious action so mechanical.

I shriek.

Little of what ensues remains truly clear in my mind.

I see a suggestion of flames.

"Stop this!" I shout at the top of my voice. "In *my* cabin! Stop this!"

The two bodies judder to a halt. Surprised jibbering. Cavatina giggles. And it occurs to me suddenly just how grotesque sexual intercourse can look.

They snatch up clothes. Say nothing, though Cavatina laughs a maniacal laugh. Perry Ellis cries low as if in pain—or perhaps he is praying.

"Get out!"

My voice seems to come from someone I have never been.

I see the flash of the eyes of Perry Ellis. I see the fangs of the tattoo on the throat of Cavatina. They scramble for the door, their clothes pressed in bundles against their bodies.

"Perry Ellis, I hope your demons make you suffer!"

My throat is raw. The intensity of my trembling frightens me.

"Cavatina—you are wicked beyond belief!"

But the two of them have escaped into the heat of the day, carrying with them the heat of their passion and the echoes of my fury.

I sense that I may faint.

I stare down at my cot: I consider trashing it or perhaps setting it afire. When my trembling ebbs, I grow very calm. I put away my groceries, and I walk briskly to my pond. I sit and watch turtles accept the gift of sun. Jacob and Marauder wade in the shallow end like boys who have skipped school. They are almost comically unaware of how my cabin has been desecrated.

I blank out images of Perry Ellis and Cavatina.

I surrender, blissfully, to the aftermath that sometimes follows an assault on one's emotions.

But the past creeps back into my thoughts like a hungry animal.

I think of a beautiful, crystalline salamander.

I think of Mr. Breyer—the days of our affair. The montage, at first, flows sweetly: those initial, innocent kisses in his science lab at the end of the school hours. And the moment, in a dark closet, feeling his lips against the nape of my neck, the kisses, his warm breath, and his hands slipping up to caress my breasts. I recall wanting to feel his body on mine. I wanted the weight of his desire to find pleasure and satisfaction in all that I could possibly offer as a woman.

But no consummation ever occurred.

No intimacy to that degree.

There never seemed to be world enough and time.

Or enough courage.

Then, in time, the inevitable: the turning.

I felt wronged.

Wronged.

And perhaps Poe's "Imp" goaded me.

Mr. Breyer kept a prized possession on his desk: a glass salamander resting atop a dark, cherry wood pedestal. It was a lovely, lovely piece; it was from Italy, I believe. He treasured it.

He often talked of the symbolic import of the salamander, its magical properties, the legends surrounding it that went back as far as Pliny.

"The salamander represents those who pass through the fires of passion and of this world without stain," he told me.

I admired his words.

Until the day they became just words.

Mr. Breyer's hypocrisy burned deep within me; the sight of his salamander—creature of fire—fueled my need for revenge.

Wronged, I was.

Wronged.

One morning, very early, before classes commenced, I smashed the salamander.

Although I never confessed to the deed, Mr. Breyer knew. In time, the whole school knew, and my tenure at Mahonia was in jeopardy.

Mr. Breyer never confronted me about my act.

I wish he had.

July 7

I stay inside.

My thermometer on the wooden clothesline post registers ninety-eight degrees by early afternoon. I have seen no sign of either Perry Ellis or Cavatina. Why do they make me so angry? The obvious reading is that I am jealous, but I sense something else.

I try to read. Mostly Emerson. The words jump around on the page. I have the jitters. I hear strange noises.

At twilight Allegra shows up alone. She is as innocently beautiful as one of those young women in Botticelli's paintings: she is Venus having stepped from the sea onto land. I offer her iced tea.

She repeats herself.

"Can we go into the swamp one night? Please. I have to see it, but not with Lucas. I have to know what he has *felt*."

I tell her absolutely not.

But her eyes plead like the eyes of my Lucas, and I relent some.

"I shall have to think about this. As I have said, the swamp is dangerous. It would be foolhardy to go there at night."

"I need to," she says. "I have no choice."

She is deep within herself, like a woman heavy with child.

I am being asked to midwife her in the birthing of darkness.

"I must think about this," I say. "Is my Lucas aware of what you ask, what you need?"

"He loves me."

That is her only response.

Hours later, I am sitting alone by my fire pit when Tevis shyly approaches to inform me that he is camping out by the pond again.

"Do you believe in the Beast?" he asks.

Had he not posed that question before?

"No," I say. "Or, rather, I think we believe what we *need* to believe."

I am neither convincing nor compelling.

Very slowly, almost gravely, he says, "Something's out there—I feel it."

I can only shrug.

I thank him again for his drawing. He says that he is doing new work.

"On the walls of Cat Bells. When I finish, I'll show you."

And for some reason I shiver when I hear his words.

July 8

This morning while I am straightening and brushing off Resurrection Fern's shabby cloak, I am stung on the wrist by a yellow jacket. They have hives at the line of demarcation between the woods and the cleared area around my cabin. These hives are small holes in the ground about as big as a quarter. If you watch carefully, you can see nearly a dozen of these nasty, winged critters fountain out of the opening, dispatched, I assume, to find food for the queen. It sounds like royal duty.

I must have disturbed one more than usual because I have rarely been stung in the past. After I put ice on the sting, I walk to the pond and scoop up a handful of slimy mud for a poultice of sorts. Back in the cabin, I feel that my arm is swelling; I can see it streaking purple and yellow.

I have been poisoned.

There is a notion in the South that, on occasion, a yellow jacket will inject a body with wise poison.

In my case, we shall see.

By afternoon, the temperature once again reaches ninety-eight.

It is almost too hot to breathe or blink one's eyes—the humidity is jungle-like, horrendous.

I am thinking strangely unkind thoughts about Allegra.

Is the wrong kind of poison coursing through me?

I feel weak and irritable.

And then I receive a visitor.

His eyes clearly showing signs that he has been crying, Perry Ellis, dressed in his Sunday clothes, stands in the doorway like an ebony mirage. His bottom lip quivers; I believe he has come to apologize.

He cups something in one hand, carefully keeping it out of sight.

I stare at him. He lowers his head.

I wish that my mothering instinct were strong enough to allow me to go to him and hold him and assure him that all is forgiven.

My head swims.

My arm throbs.

Something wild and hateful—beastly—rises within me.

I hiss at him: "You disgust me!"

His body jerks as if he has been slugged.

That he takes my words, that he does not fight back, torches my emotions.

"Just go!"

He says nothing. His face crumples. He sobs.

I advance close to him.

"Go off and crucify yourself like your Jesus. You do not deserve to live—you or Cavatina. You are children of lustful demons."

I slap at his shoulder. Then, I, too, am crying.

"Go!"

He turns and stumbles out.

But in moments he returns and places something on the floor of my cabin before disappearing into the hellish heat of the day.

Minutes later, I pick up the object.

It is a dark wood carving of a soft-shelled turtle—beautifully wrought.

July 9

They have the scent of me.

Pheromones, I believe.

On this very muggy morning, I am stung a second time. The back of my neck throbs. I go for ice and pond mud again. Late afternoon I shall wait for the yellow jackets to return to their hives, then pour a cup of gasoline down each hole and block their escape with a rock.

I can foster no fellowship with the living menaces of Nature.

By early afternoon, the second sting is burning like fire. I go to Deep Kill Creek and soak a wash cloth and drape it on my neck. It helps some. When I return to my cabin, I find Cavatina and Jenny.

I suspect more apologies are in the air.

I invite them out of the furnace, but Cavatina—cowardly tramp that she is—pets and dotes on Marauder by the fire pit.

Jenny comes in and asks me to forgive Cavatina.

She talks about the young woman's wretched home life. She talks, her bad teeth and sad eyes difficult for me to look at. And yet, I sense that she is honest and sincere.

I interrupt her at one point to say,

"Why are you doing this?"

At first, she is diminished. Then she recovers, blinks away her timidity and thrusts out her chin. But she quakes as she speaks.

"You see," she says, "I love her. I love Cavatina, dearly."

Love and poison.

I smile and tell her that while I can appreciate her feelings, I would rather not say anything about Cavatina—I am too angry.

I do not want her in my sight.

Woman and girl leave.

In the dying light of day, I gas three yellow jacket hives. I feel a curious satisfaction.

Although there is an evening shower, replete with lightning, the storm barely cools the air.

I sit up and read Poe.

His words thunder in my thoughts.

July 10

My stings are not as swollen and painful today.
My Lucas stops by. I could hear him singing as he approached my cabin—the sound of an angel winging into my heart. Oddly enough, he sings a 1950s tune my mother liked: "The Little White Cloud That Cried" by Johnnie Ray. He stays only long enough to drink a glass of iced tea and to tell me how much Allegra admires me and wants to be my friend. He works hard in her behalf.

I am conflicted.

Apparently he knows about Cavatina and Perry Ellis.

He tells me not to be so upset about what happened, for they are barely more than children.

Before he leaves, I say, "Promise you will never leave me."

He smiles his magnificent smile.

"Jessica Love, I will *never* leave you, dear sister."

The day is not quite so hot as the previous ones. Thunder swings north and west of my cabin tonight as I lie in bed and try to decide what it is that I must do.

Near midnight, I think I hear the movement of some massive animal up beyond the pond. Can it be the Beast? I hear something like a growl or a monstrous, piggish grunt. I imagine that it shakes my cabin.

Is the Beast calling?

Or is it the huge, unforgiving phantom of my life?

July 11

It is a warm, dry, breezy Sunday morning.

Jacob and Marauder are listless. In Sweet River, Christians, no doubt, are waking and convincing themselves as best they can that there is a savior in their lives.

I know better. They must save themselves.

I assume that wherever Perry Ellis is this morning he is praying.

I assume that wherever Cavatina is she is not.

Tevis, I believe, is in Cat Bells casting his art upon the walls.

I sit now in my kitchen with a volume of Poe in my lap, and I play a game with myself. I pretend that the gods or some "on-looking numinous spirit" guides me as I open the text at random—is there a tale that needs to come into my presence?

"Mesmeric Revelation" is on the page I turn to.

I smile at the coincidence, for I woke thinking that I needed revelation of some kind.

A smattering of yellow jackets, now hiveless, buzz near my doorway. I am their nemesis. I tell them to go sting Resurrection Fern—she can handle the pain.

I read Poe's tale with my first cup of coffee. I am drawn to a description of the person mesmerized: one who "… perceives, with keenly refined perception, and through channels supposed unknown, matters beyond the scope of the physical organs.…" My breathing accelerates. The one mesmerized exclaims, "All created things are but the thoughts of God."

Well, of course, that depends on your definition of "God."

I finish the tale, and I wonder with Poe: do certain individuals address us from the regions of the shadows?

Quite suddenly, I know what I must do.

I will go tell Allegra that she is welcome to come to my cabin tomorrow evening.

July 12

Idreamed that the painful cries attendant upon childbirth filled my cabin, filled my woods. In my dream, I stumbled out under a sky swirling with stars and braced against a wind blowing down from the desolation of the moon. Someone's blood screamed into my face.

The mothering night called for my help.

Must I nurse into being what wants to come?

I fought through my fear to the dark miracle hidden out of the swing of the possible.

It was Resurrection Fern. Mama scarecrow animated through suffering.

Then I stared.

Bathed in steam, a hideous thing escaped from beneath her gown, a thing too grotesque to look at for more than a glimpse. But in that fleeting moment, I saw a creature blink into the world, wailing in protest.

Then I winced; terror rose within me.

The eyes of the tiny beast were the eyes of my Lucas.

For most of the day, that dream gripped my body, my thoughts, like a case of the flu. Was the god of nightmares playing cruel tricks?

I shook it off as well as I might.

I readied for my evening with Allegra.

Sunset arrives. Thunderstorms march just to the north and west as if they feel a need to avoid my property. Do they sense that madness is the *genius loci*?

It seems that nothing else is stirring as Allegra enters my

cabin trailing secrets from beyond the veil. If she is a creature spawned by a god, then it is one of the darkest gods in
the pantheon. I greet the shattering intensity of her eyes. She
has brought her violin. When she embraces me, she awakens a
nameless force in some unreachable part of my body, a primordial bent. In her presence, I am frightened of myself.

She possesses the fascination of the abyss.

We sit. She asks for a cup of hot tea, and though it feels much
too warm this evening, I oblige her. Seated next to her at my
table, I feel the existence of spiritual influences. I hope it is not
too obvious that I am uncomfortable.

She begins to narrate her life, and I find it extremely difficult
to listen. At one point, she explains that she was named after
the illegitimate daughter of Lord Byron. At another point, my
kerosene lantern dims, and I hear her voice echo to me from
far away: "I've never known my father," she says. "Sometimes I
pretend that I was fathered by a ghost."

This is my dilemma: I am thankful that Allegra has given
my Lucas a life, and yet I am jealous to a pathological degree,
an emotion strong enough to usher in murderous thoughts. But
I am also in awe of this strange young woman, perhaps even
terrified of her. Why was she called back from death? Is there
something of the supernatural in her? Or the numinous?

She reaches for my hand and whispers,

"I was raped and buried by the Beast."

I tremble. My teeth softly chatter.

Posthumous Allegra.

How many forms of darkness have possessed her?

My tea water boils, and Allegra plays her violin—I hear
nothing but a dirge. Shadows take over my cabin. I feel that
I am frozen in a painting by Caravaggio. Shadows define our
boundaries. And for the first time ever, I truly believe that the
Beast may well exist, may well be waiting for us at the edge of
the swamp.

Passion and detachment—Allegra wears both.

In the hollows of her cheeks, I see death growing within her.

When I lift the tea kettle, I have to fight to keep from scalding her eyes.

If she were a delicate, glass figurine, I would smash her.

She sugars her tea and leans over it, breathing in the steam as if she is a seer. She takes one sip, then her eyes seek another world: she asks for a pencil and several sheets of paper.

Again, I oblige.

I stand and keep my distance. It appears that she has fallen into a trance. Then her upper body begins to quake as if she is freezing to death: her eyes roll up—her histrionics are so exaggerated as to be almost comical.

But I am not laughing.

She snuffles loudly, weirdly. She begins to write.

All I want is to leave. I cannot bear the presence of this young woman. I suddenly see myself as a figure of failed covenant, and yet what was my agreement and with whom? I came to my property in self-exile. Why is it that people cannot allow me my solitude?

I stay.

I am a devil.

But I repent nothing.

Allegra, or whatever, whoever possesses her, attacks the sheets of paper, etching upon them with a childish scrawl. My hands trembling, I pick up the first of the sheets and I read....

"I am from beyond the grave."

. . .

"Of death, only I have knowledge."

Allegra continues to write. She hunches forward as if bracing herself against a strong wind from out of the everywhere.

I read from a second sheet....

"Do not mourn Death and Memory."

. . .

"The Beast is the only guide to Beauty."

I feel something snap within. In a fury, I wad up the sheets and scream, "Stop this! Stop it!"

But the one mesmerized continues.

From above my door I wrest my double-bladed hatchet.

Voices of blood cry out like demons in my spirit.

I raise my weapon. I feel nothing within the insanity of my nothingness.

With all my strength, I swing down.

I bury the blade of my madness into my table top.

The shadows splinter.

Allegra ceases. She shakes free. She rises to the surface of reality.

Nausea sweeps through me. I heave with dry sobs.

I cannot move. I cannot avoid Allegra as she comes to me and embraces me and whispers, "It's time for us to go to the swamp."

I shake my head. I must refuse her call, but in the end I shall not be able to. And when I have calmed myself, I lift my lantern. I tell Marauder and Jacob not to follow us.

Like a patient reader of my narrative, Allegra holds my hand.

Our vesperal walk must, I know, remain rigorously unknowable.

Except for this: only one of us can return alive.

I lead her as if I know the way. We follow an ancient path and, beyond us, lies the great Nahollo Swamp symbolic of human kind's desperate struggle for survival. Lightning dances on the horizon to the west. Distant thunder. We walk into a vast solitude that exists, indifferently, with vivid contrasts: evil and beneficence, beauty and ugliness and the intricately interwoven strands of life and death.

Night insects chorus. But I imagine more: the intense actuality of sound that my body amplifies. Do I hear, far away, ghouls and insane howlings? I slow and turn and raise my lantern into the eyes of Allegra—she is whispering. I lean in to hear her words.

"I want to be the poet of my own death. I'm drawing it into my life like words." She pauses. Then continues. "Do you know what transmutation is? Lucas does. He has the voice of endlessness. He sings of eternity."

I shove roughly at her shoulder.

"Stop that! Stop, please!"

Have I taken her too far? We are soon a quarter of a mile from the cabin. Our path snakes through shallow water at the edge of a copse of giant cypresses; their gnarled knees try to trip us. I hear an owl hoot as if amazed that anyone could be intruding.

And I feel that someone or some *thing* is watching us.

The night mists into a grayish miasma of primitive forces.

We have entered a realm that has lost its soul if ever it had one.

In the crazed yet velvet swirl of my thoughts, I think of Thoreau and a few words that apply so aptly: "... I seek the darkest wood, the thickest and most interminable ... I enter the swamp as a sacred place, a *sanctum sanctorum.*"

Is it truly possible to worship wildness?

I tighten my grip on Allegra's hand.

I smell her menstrual blood.

She stumbles along like a sleepwalker, her eyes open, seeing things, I assume, that I would never wish to see. She speaks again, but her voice has changed—no longer hers—the voice of the swamp, perhaps. *A voice that belongs dead.*

"We're on the track that's lost its way," she says.

I feel an old belonging to those words, for I realize that what I am doing is unforgiveable.

We walk on, and I am listening to the darkness, but Allegra is hearing voices beyond the human—voices she has prepared to hear—and I cannot possibly know what they are saying.

I glance now at my feet where something has slithered through the shallows. I can feel Allegra's warm breath on the back of my neck. I pull her with me back to more solid ground.

Where someone blocks our passage.

I cry out in surprise.

Night birds take wing.

As if on cue, there is lightning and thunder and a hot wind.

My lantern sprays across the small, resolute figure of Sister Speakes.

"Go back," she says, tonelessly. "This is the track of death rising. It leads to a place where no one returns alive."

I say nothing. I meet the woman's eyes, the wisdom, the knowing sunken there like buried treasure. Allegra is silent, too, yet her breathing is almost a determined growl. I can feel that despite the warning she has no choice but to continue.

Just as mysteriously as she appeared, Sister Speakes turns and walks away, swallowed at last by the wildness of the swamp.

It is time for me to do what I must do.

I tug Allegra close to me. I embrace her. Then, in a spontaneous, unexpected act, I kiss her on the cheek. I push her forward.

She goes her way.

She begins to call the Beast.

I swing around in the direction of my cabin, clinging to a frenzied hope that I have not lost my way.

I turn down the light of my lantern completely.

The near total darkness is strangely exciting.

I head back alone, pausing only when I hear a crashing in the thicket of the impenetrable swamp.

I continue on.

I do not stop even when Allegra's screams tear at my body like claws.

In my cabin, my lantern re-lit, I lay my head on my splintered table, and I fight a welling of emotion: *what have I done?* I raise my eyes. The sight of Allegra's violin saddens me. Now I must rehearse what to say to my Lucas. Where will I find the words? I whisper into the shadows within me:

"I did what she asked."

I did what she asked.

Solitude, my only companion, emerges from the emptiness surrounding me, a gentle giant, mute, the air of his aloneness impossible to breathe. He wants to speak; I think he wants to console me. A greater solitude hovers up among the stars, far beyond my cabin. Does my essential self wander there? Sorrow smothers my need to respond. Solitude grunts and whimpers. Madness herself lurks at my door.

Or is it someone else?

I stare.

But I cannot believe my eyes.

Allegra, her hands extended, staggers into my cabin.

There is no life in her eyes. She does not belong to herself. As she reaches for me, her voice, low and mechanical, seems to come from her chest as if there is a radio implanted there. Her lips do not move.

"Talk," she says. "Ask questions."

I shake my head.

"What should I ask?"

"Ask about death. Ask whether I'm dead."

"No," I say. "You must not die. You must *not*."

My thoughts are flooded with images of my Lucas, of the unbearable sorrow he would experience.

Allegra trembles.

"I've been frightened," she murmurs. "So terribly frightened."

"I can help you," I say.

I hold her wrists.

But I feel no pulse.

A smile flickers at one corner of her lips.

"I'm contented," she says.

And then collapses to the floor.

I shake at her shoulders. I slap at her cheeks.

I call out, demanding that she live.

But her body is as lifeless as that of Resurrection Fern.

July 13

I believe that it is approaching dawn.

I cannot remember much of what occurred a few hours ago: rushing to my Lucas; his return to my cabin; his fear, his anguish, his disbelief. He did not, I seem to recall, even ask questions. He could barely breathe through frenzied sobs.

He lifted his beloved into his arms and hurried to his trailer.

I held back.

Nothing to be done.

Death crosses the boundaries of dying.

I must wait on this side of life.

Alone for now.

And then I must grieve with my Lucas.

July 14

Yesterday passed with hours of an all-consuming numbness. I ate nothing. I fed Marauder and Jacob.

No one visited.

I read nothing.

I barely left my cabin.

The temperature today will soar into the upper nineties. No rain on the horizon.

My Lucas will believe that there is no hope in sight, but I shall give him all my love, and when the time is right, he will find his song again.

I must give him space. He must greet Solitude, mute visitor, and enter the depths of himself, for there is no other way to resurrect himself.

I have made a decision.

I shall tell him that the Beast is to blame.

July 15

I do not want my Lucas to hate me.

If he asks how his Allegra died, I shall tell him that she was frightened to death. The ghost of our father was right: the Beast must be destroyed. My Lucas should now be even more intent upon revenge.

The Beast *must* be destroyed.

It does not matter what I truly believe.

The inextinguishable flame of my love for my Lucas will thaw him out from the frozen depths of his grief.

Late morning, I wade barefoot in Deep Kill Creek to escape the terrible heat. Marauder and Jacob join me—the water level lowers some each day.

By twilight, I am nearly crazy with a desire to go to my Lucas. He needs me. There is a burial to be arranged, I assume. Who else, I wonder, knows what has occurred?

I am having trouble keeping my thoughts clear.

Near midnight I awaken.

I hear singing.

July 16

I am a funeral in my brain.

Emily would understand—Mr. Walt, too.

Yes, of course, I know that Dickinson wrote, "I *felt* a funeral in my brain," but somehow those words are not strong enough for me. I sense that I have become a living ritual—a death ritual—and that I am burying myself.

This morning a muggy fog haunts my woods and wails at the walls of my cabin. I find myself listening for something: is it the beat of the wings of suffering? I do not know. I also find myself thinking much about the people in my small life. Was it not Henry James who wrote that one should never say he knows the last word about any human heart?

I put on my hiking clothes and head out into the fog. I imagine that Miss Emily Dickinson, ghost lady, accompanies me. As we walk, I can hear her whisper some of her most resonant opening lines:

"Again—his voice is at the door—"

…

"The only Ghost I ever saw"

…

"One need not be a Chamber—to be Haunted—"

…

"We grow accustomed to the Dark—"

…

I am no spiritualist, but I begin to think that Dickinson, perhaps, was. Up near Cat Bells I bid her goodbye. The fog claims her, poet in white carrying her poetry of whiteness.

Gracious goodness, I do not want to traffic with the dead. I do, however, accept that I must wander in the country of absence. My Lucas is there seeking a presence that has transformed into a no longer can be.

By the time I return to my cabin, the fog has lifted. I sense that the gods are disappointed in me. I should not have taken Allegra into the swamp to meet the death that had departed from within her and waited for her to come.

I make myself coffee. I do not drink it.

Minutes pass before the beautiful voice of my Lucas shakes the funk from my brain. Am I only imagining that voice? No, it is real. He is approaching my cabin. I listen carefully, but I cannot make out the words of the song he is singing, only that the tune seems sad and yet hopeful, almost forward-looking.

I rise to meet the smiling face of my Lucas.

He braces his hands against either side of the door and ends the song with a flourish. Warm sparks fountain from my heart.

"Jessica Love," he says. "I told you that someone had promised never to leave."

"That song," I say, "is not one I know."

"It's Allegra's song."

I hesitate.

Marauder is barking his bark that signals the arrival of a stranger.

I whisper through the paralysis of my breath.

"Who is there?"

I stare at my Lucas.

He strides to me. Hugs me. Turns and leaves my cabin saying, "You'll see."

I mutter something.

"No ghosts, please."

There is an inchoate whirl in the doorway. My Lucas is pulling gently at someone.

Then he is practically shouting.

"She's alive and well. Look here. Look here."

I cannot believe my eyes.

"Oh, no," I murmur.

"My singing did it. Do you see? My singing brought her back."

Allegra staggers stiffly through the doorway. My Lucas continues to chortle in bliss.

But he is wrong, wrong, wrong.

The young woman with glassy, unblinking eyes, the eyes of a waking serpent, is most certainly not alive.

July 17

L̲ast evening there was a brief shower. I was thankful for it somewhat—the cooling effect of it—and yet it added to my depression. Not even the reassuring wisdom of Emerson could dissipate my gloom.

When I closed my eyes in bed and tried to sleep, all I could see was the empty face of Allegra with death rising to fill it like putrid water.

This morning I am better. Stronger.

I ache for my Lucas, but I must not reject his world or his self-delusion, for if I do I shall lose him forever. I see now that he will need to be resurrected a second time.

Around noon, I am pleased to find him at my door. He asks that I read tonight; he plans to ask everyone to come—to celebrate the return of Allegra.

Of course, I cannot say no.

I cannot.

His smile transports him away.

Afternoon brings another brief shower.

Tiny rainbows fill my woods.

I shall be upbeat this evening for my Lucas and for the Good Faces, one and all.

I have fixed up more than usual, donning my best school dress, mauve in color, a strand of pearls for a touch of class; and two extravagancies: white gloves and a coating of red lipstick I found at Wal-Mart—it is called, "Devastation," a silly name, and yet as I drink in my image in my mirror, I feel almost pretty, almost desirable, almost wicked. I giggle at myself until I have to bite my lip. I am covering great pain that grows from many sources. I am putting on an act. Playing a role.

They arrive like wild animals approaching cautiously from a forest.

I shake my head when I notice that Resurrection Fern is naked—two pink balloons bob as her bare breasts. Oh, my. It must be the work of Cavatina. She is holding Jenny's hand, and when she sees me she calls out, "Hell, yes! Miss DeGresse, you look hot, woman!"

"Thank you," I say.

Tevis has brought his friend, "Skylar,"—known as "Sky"— who is small and thin with long, blond hair. He seems an orphaned waif from a Dickens novel. When I look more closely, I note that he is sickly with large, watery eyes and a hesitant smile. A boy fairy, he is quiet and stays quite close to Tevis.

My Lucas escorts Allegra to one of my chairs.

She looks ghastly.

From out of the everywhere, a snippet from Coleridge's *Ancient Mariner* seizes my thoughts:

Her lips were red, her looks were free,
Her locks were yellow as gold:
Her skin was as white as leprosy,
The Nightmare Life-in-Death was she....

Allegra is among us in body only. Life-in-Death indeed.

And yet, my Lucas is beaming.

Much to my surprise, Perry Ellis shows up; he is carrying Resurrection Fern's loop of new rope. Does he plan to lasso demonic spirits? He seems almost as dead as Allegra. He sits next to Lucas and as far from Cavatina as possible. He is, I believe, terrified of Allegra.

It is a strange, ethereal group. When everyone is seated, and I peruse them in the combined light of the fire pit and my lantern, I shiver. Can I go on? I glance at my Lucas. His eyes overflow with hope. Yes, I shall go on.

The stars that twinkle down upon us are already dead. So, we, the living, must shine on as if the universe is *not* thoroughly indifferent to us. Tevis helps me pour glasses of wine, and before I begin to read, my Lucas stands and pleasantly shocks me with a toast:

"To Jessica Love, the one who has brought us all together."

They cheer.

Am I the keeper of those who fall?

It is a question that I must live, for I have no answer.

I feel giddy with false elation.

I read Dickinson's #1260, perhaps the greatest poem ever written on human loss. It begins …

Because that you are going
And never coming back
And I, however absolute
May overlook your Track—
Because that Death is final,
However first it be,
This instant be suspended
Above Mortality—

I ramble on about the lines, re-living my days as a teacher, about how the persona of the poem stands tall in the face of the man she loves, a man who is dying. She displays strength beyond any comforting bereavement.

I fear that I am making my remarks too personal.

Is there no one to stop me?

Thankfully, they have turned their attention to each other: Jenny to Cavatina, Tevis to Sky, and my Lucas to Allegra. As to Perry Ellis—a demon perhaps of whiteness has him in its grip.

I fight for their attention.

"Please listen," I say. "There is something I must share with you about poetry and literature … about what a life of reading can mean to you."

Goodness, my sentences riot.

What am I talking about?

I overhear myself mention that reading has kept me from being lonely, that it puts me in contact with worlds other than my own, that I can enjoy the process in solitude, that it deepens my sense of self, and that it helps me to belong to myself.

I talk of Emerson, Thoreau, Poe, Hawthorne, Melville,

Whitman, and Dickinson as if they are old friends who have allowed me to be a member of their tribe, a tribe I respect and revere. They share with me the compelling process of literary creation.

Dear me, what else have I said?

Suddenly I hear my Good Faces applauding.

They thank me.

They rise and leave.

But I ask myself: Will my night ever end?

July 18

This morning my thoughts are so scattered.

I ask myself, for example, whether I have ever thanked Perry Ellis for the exquisite turtle he carved for me.

I think, in unrelated terms, about Allegra's session of automatic writing—it confused and frightened me to see what she penned.

I think about last night's gathering of my Good Faces: the ones alive and the ones almost alive; the ones who have created eros and the ones who have destroyed it.

After feeding Marauder and Jacob, I head out for the pond, but my thoughts are stuck on Allegra like strips of Velcro. Her nightmare life-in-death is shrouded in an unending dream of nothingness.

My Lucas has entered that dream and refuses to wake up.

Pleased I am to be greeted by Tevis. He and Sky have pitched their tent beside the pond. Sky is still asleep. He, according to Tevis, had a good time at my reading, but his condition renders him easily tired. I do not press to find what it is Sky suffers from—if Tevis feels compelled to tell me, he will. I am gladdened that Tevis has a friend, that he is not as lonely as I feared.

Is this handsome, young, sensitive poet of a soul *my* friend?

I like to think he is.

I do not, however, quite understand what he is doing in my life.

He and I talk about last night.

"Cavatina and Jenny," he says, "they seem like a good couple."

I believe he is probing for my reaction to their relationship: Do I approve of it?

"Jenny is a loving soul," I say, "but she needs to understand that Cavatina is utterly selfish, concerned only with her … her own *needs*."

"She's young," says Tevis. "She's very young."

My jaw stiffens.

"She's vile."

"But you care for her—I can tell."

I look away. On the edges of the pond, turtles have emerged to worship or to be worshiped by the sun.

I shake my head.

"I wish Perry Ellis would stay away," I say, and I think I mean it.

"Cavatina draws him. He can't resist."

"He is foolish. So terribly foolish."

Tevis pauses thoughtfully; he seems, in the moment, much older than he is.

"I think … I'm afraid he might harm himself, you know, physically."

I hear genuine concern in his tone, but I deflect it with a smile.

"No. No, he is merely a boy trying on the metaphorical clothing of a man. He is trying to play the part. He is hurt. I made him feel ashamed. His belief system makes him feel worthless. Demons keep him company. But he would not, I assure you, wreak havoc upon his body. His soul or spirit, yes. His body, no. He is too proud of it."

I sense that Tevis does not agree. I am relieved when he changes the subject.

"Are you going," he says, "to insist that your brother seek medical help for Allegra?"

The question nearly takes my breath away.

I stare into his dark, lovely eyes.

"No," I say. "My Lucas is not ready for that." I hesitate, for I do not know what I mean. "He does not see what the rest of us see. He is blind to it. He would die before he would let her go."

I feel my heart beating much too rapidly. I have no idea whether Tevis can make any sense of my words. I am not certain that I do.

"Was it the Beast?" he says.

"There is no Beast," I snap.

I fold my arms against my breasts and walk away a few yards. He follows. I smell the fragrance of his shadow.

"What would you think," he says, "if I took Sky to see Sister Speakes?"

I skid into the turn of his surprising question.

When I do not respond, he explains that his friend has been given no hope by medical doctors and that alternative medicine might be worth exploring. He confesses that he loves Sky and would do anything for him.

I find where my voice is hiding, and I murmur, "Do what you must do."

He smiles weakly. He takes my hand.

"I want to show you my cave painting. Come."

I am astonished.

We are inside, some thirty yards from the entrance to Cat Bells. The air is cool and intimately moist. The spray from the high-beam flashlight discovers a triptych on one wall, replete with human-like figures and a massive snake depicted much in the primitive style and manner of the Australian aborigines.

"This is my revelation," says Tevis.

I do not quite follow what he could possibly mean, nor do I understand his technical description of how he managed to paint upon the sweating, blond rock surface. It does not matter, of course. I quietly thrill to the artist's passion. I find myself hoping that my Lucas has or soon will view this hidden masterpiece.

"Do you see what I've tried to capture?" Tevis asks.

Why on earth I nod that I do is beyond me.

The far left section of the mural—each section is three to four feet high—shows nine black, stick-like human figures dancing, two or three holding spears.

Tevis probes.

"Do their movements translate as joy or fear?"

Both is what I think. My eye is drawn more to the tail of the monstrous serpent: it is tricked out in blocky segments—black, white and cave-blond. I begin to see the creature as an Edenic source of terror.

Tevis folds into silence. I sense that he is watching me in my deep looking.

The second section features the slithering sweep of the thick body of the snake. Two stick figures appear ready to attack the intruder, but fail to release their spears. Even more arrestingly, at the top of the painting a figure is depicted as he falls into a treacherous, V-shaped abyss.

This is obviously a chronicle of a nightmare. Something personal, I assume.

The third section concludes what seems an allegorical narrative. The giant snake, its triangular head frozen in the act of spewing venom harmlessly into the air, is about to flee the scene. More central to this section is a large, more muscular and complete human figure holding a small serpent aloft while standing upon the head of another, crushing it with his heel.

Clearly an aura of triumph emerges.

At the bottom of the painting, stick figures pray and appear to experience a thanksgiving.

I turn to Tevis and whisper, "This is extraordinary."

His eyes scan the painting as if seeing into the wall itself.

"This has been my life—this arrived as a gift to explain myself to myself."

"Is it too private to share—the something here that you won over?"

He seems relieved to confess that for many years he has suffered from a severe anxiety disorder. Medication and psychotherapy have helped little.

"But art—and being in this cave—well, I've learned that I can come to terms with the beasts within. My beasts."

When we leave Cat Bells, thunder prowls all around us. But there is no rain. No respite from the intense heat. Nature retains her indifference.

I thank Tevis and say goodbye.

I walk on some inner path of possible creations.

The life of my Lucas suddenly fills the entire canvas of my thoughts.

July 19

I have taken the ball that serves as the face of Resurrection Fern and have given her more feminine eyes and a much nicer smile. In addition, I have removed her large breasts. From my closet, I select a school dress in a shade of cinnamon, quite pretty and long with a rather elegant line. Then I decide that Fern needs a hat. From among a few of my boxes of vintage hats, some of which belonged to my mother, I come upon a felt suit hat with netting—a "Marion Valle." It happens also to be cinnamon in color, complemented with orange and green feathers. I spray Fern with some perfume that possesses a hint of lilac.

My lady scarecrow now has a touch of class this morning.

I add a white purse and a string of pearls to her ensemble.

She beams, or, I imagine her to.

Mid-morning, before the dragon-fire heat of day begins to roar, I wander up by the pond. I long to see turtles. At one end, shaded under a pair of willows, Tevis and Sky have spread out a blanket; they appear engaged in conversation. I wave at them, but I shall not disturb them.

I continue on to Deep Kill Creek where I see Marauder and Jacob on a sandbar oblivious to the agony of human life. Then I hear splashing. I look farther up the creek, and I immediately press my fingers over my eyes. Cavatina and Jenny are thigh deep in the stream and more naked than Adam and Eve.

Gracious goodness!

But they do seem to be enjoying themselves.

I start to turn away when I notice a dark smudge of movement on the bank not far from the skinny dippers—it is Perry

Ellis, murdered by lust and shame and, likely, surrounded by invisible demons of envy.

I feel deep sorrow for him.

At the same time, he disgusts me.

In a bit of a funk, I return to my cabin where, unexpectedly, Allegra and my Lucas are seated at my table.

"You accepting callers?" says my Lucas.

"Oh, yes. Yes, of course," I say.

I pour some iced tea. Allegra drinks none of hers. In fact, she keeps her hands in her lap. Her face is a mask of emptiness. I do not believe that she can blink her eyes. She does not speak. She does, however, issue a grunt now and then. Is she communicating? I see that she is terribly thin and pale. The skin on her cheeks appears to be desiccating.

I find her presence most unsettling.

Recalling my conversation with Tevis yesterday, I seize the moment and suggest that it might be a good idea, now that Allegra has recovered some from her shock in the swamp, to have her visit a doctor to make certain all is well.

My Lucas bristles.

"She's fine. She's back. Can't you see that?"

I pull my head into the shell of myself and murmur, "Is she truly getting better?"

My Lucas practically shouts his response: "She's contented. That's good enough."

They depart.

And something begins to tick within me—something horrible.

I struggle through the remainder of the day.

At twilight, I feel a curious need to embrace the wonder of that marvelous painting on the wall of Cat Bells—I long to witness a narrative of recovery and triumph.

When I arrive at the cave, I hear voices.

Inside, Tevis has on his large flashlight, and he is talking about his painting. Allegra and my Lucas are with him. I start to retreat, but Tevis insists that I stay.

Moments later, with a light of his own, my Lucas guides Allegra farther into the cavern. Tevis and I follow. I listen, distractedly, to Tevis and my Lucas sharing observations about rock structures, formations and related issues. At one point, we reach a ledge. Beyond and beneath is a black eternity of time and space like Thoreau's bottomless pond, only deeper. Tevis kicks a small rock into the opening.

I listen.

But I never hear the rock strike firmament or water.

I turn away, for it feels hideous to be so close to the horrors of an unimaginable accident should one fall into that abyss.

Allegra and my Lucas seem not in the least unnerved by it.

Tevis manifests a healthy respect for the fearsome phenomenon.

I excuse myself. The sight of Allegra and my Lucas together brushes over me with morbid colors. Together they seem a sacrilege to love; my affection for my Lucas must respond to their unholiness. That much is certain.

Back near my cabin, I pause to speak to Resurrection Fern.

"I cannot bear this," I say. "I cannot."

July 20

Heart Laid Bare … again.

I have seen no one all day.

In the smothering dark of evening I light my fire pit and sip at a glass of wine and scratch at Marauder's back with my toes.

Deep inside me nothing is growing; everything is burning. Snakes of flames slither through my thoughts.

I cannot let my Lucas continue to embrace such self-delusion. I cannot.

July 21

As I gather the materials I need for my act of love, I am pleased that the air just now at sunrise is so warm. It is appropriate. The ground beneath my feet seems to pant; the hot breath of eternity rises around me.

Yes, I am desperate.

Wagnerian arias of redemption play as ear worms in my head.

I head out for the darkened trailer where my Lucas and his Allegra are locked in their unnatural sleep. I have what I need: kerosene and matches and an admixture of courage and madness—more madness than courage.

I tell myself that if I dribble a trail of kerosene completely around the trailer and then set a match to it that the conflagration will be inextinguishable. There will be a few moments of horror, but the love that is death rather than love will be no more. If my Lucas returns as a ghost, he will thank me.

As I approach the trailer, I realize that I am being watched.

Someone is near.

Glancing to my left, I see Perry Ellis atop Jacob, that new rope as a rein. Although he cannot see me, he senses where I am, and I assume that, somehow, he knows what I am planning.

His presence fires my anger.

"Go on away from here!" I shout. "No one wants you around!"

He kicks at Jacob's flank and heads past me up towards the pond.

Why did he not try to stop me?

Will no one stop me?

I stand—for how long I do not know—and fight back tears.

Then I take a deep breath and unscrew the cap of the kerosene can.

I imagine flames that shall burn forever.

And I hear a voice. And I hear someone running.

I turn to see the approach of Tevis.

"Don't!" he calls out. "Miss Jessica, don't!"

There is a blaze of intense concern in his eyes. Then he reaches my side, breathing heavily, quaking, searching my face as first light dawns.

I tremble.

I feel my lips quivering.

Words cower in my throat.

I cannot speak.

I cannot move.

July 22

Birds are active this morning because I have put out seed and water—ironically, near Resurrection Fern. They know that I have no cat, only a lazy dog and a visiting mule. I like two cardinals, a male and female, that arrive, as well as a number of smaller birds, grayish in color. All that gather seem happy and chirpy in their cautious flitting.

Songs with wings.

There is a hummingbird, too, that seeks out my dying lantanas. He treads oceans of air, thrumming spectacularly. I think to myself that my love for my Lucas is also a hovering.

It seems destined never to rest.

How could I possibly have sought to end his life?

Tevis is worried about me.

So am I.

I receive a letter from Aunt Julia's lawyer.

She has passed.

He informs me that my mother wishes to come live with me—am I agreeable? If so, arrangements will be pursued.

I feel empty.

I write back immediately that I shall comply with her wishes.

When I finish writing the letter, I continue to feel empty.

In truth, I give no thought to accommodations for the one who is destined to arrive.

July 23

In a letter to Thomas Wentworth Higginson, Emily Dickinson once wrote:

"The Sailor cannot see the North,
but knows the Needle can."

I sense, however, that *my* inner compass or direction finder has broken. I truly wonder who I am these days. Along one of my paths at dawn I stop, turn, and frown back at the woman I was moments ago.

I do not want to see my mother.

I try to adjust my eyes to a future with her in it—and I fail.

Having struggled through the morning and feeling enervated, I go down for an early afternoon nap. Before I can fall asleep, the heat and silence are shattered by shouts and screams. It is Cavatina. Her words hammer at my ears.

"You're a fucking bitch! Keep the fuck away from me! I can't stand the sight of you! Creepy bitch!"

There is more. But I concentrate on not hearing as I clamber to the door of my cabin where Cavatina, sweaty and locked in fury, her teeth gritted, rushes past me, seething.

"I don't care if she is my fuck sister—she doesn't *own* my ass. She can't control what I do. Why is she so fucking jealous?"

At first she does not seem even to notice I am there.

I pull her to my table, sit her down, and pour her some iced tea. We talk. Mostly, I listen. This is a lover's spat, I gather, centered on Cavatina's off- and on-again relationship with Perry Ellis. Jenny wants Cavatina all to herself.

The conflict is as old as the mythos of eros.

Once her venting at Jenny has been exhausted, Cavatina

grows silent. She lets me wash her face with a cold rag. She lets me hold her and stroke her hair. I remind myself that, in many ways, she is still a child.

I begin to share my threadbare wisdom concerning relationships, but along the way, I shift the subject to Allegra. I wonder what Cavatina thinks of what has happened to her sister. I wonder who all knows what condition Allegra is in.

"Why," I ask, "is no one checking on her? Is no one worried about her?"

Cavatina snorts. As usual, she deflects anything regarding the possibility that some family member cares anything about her or Allegra.

"When my pathetic mother gets back from Florida, I'll tell her Allegra has eloped. That'll be the end of that."

I am shocked and saddened.

But I am secretly pleased that Allegra's future is largely in the hands of my Lucas.

Her composure restored, Cavatina leaves after another fifteen or twenty minutes. We do not discuss Perry Ellis. Perhaps there is nothing to be said.

Not another hour passes before Jenny shows up at my door.

I brace myself for her side of things.

"I want to take her away," she says, maintaining that Cavatina needs some stability in her daily existence. I have to stifle a chuckle in the face of that understatement. But I offer neither an opinion nor consolation.

Jenny weeps unabashedly.

I locate a handkerchief for her. Through tears and quivering lips, she exclaims, "I don't have a life without her."

Which I am sure is true.

I pour her a glass of iced tea, but she does not drink it.

I have nothing else for her.

Could it be that I want her to end her involvement with Cavatina?

Minutes later she thanks me—for what, I do not know—and shuffles out into the scalding heat.

I try again, unsuccessfully, to nap.

Twilight falls.

I want to go to my Lucas.

I want Allegra out of his world.

With a glass of wine in hand, I sit by my fire pit, a volume of Whitman in my lap. I cannot read, and thus it is that I am relieved to receive still another visitor: Tevis.

"How are you?" he says.

He is like the good son looking in on his ailing mother.

I am touched.

He shares a glass of wine with me. We talk. He has seen Perry Ellis on the edge of the swamp.

"He's not in good shape, you know, mentally, emotionally."

I nod.

"He has a broken heart," I say. "He will survive it."

Tevis, however, is not as certain of it as I am. But he has other worries as well: Sky and her health. And so he tells me that he's taking his friend to Montgomery tonight to see his mother. He will return in the morning. What he does not say is that he wants to see again how I am doing—evaluate my sanity.

I say to him, "You got yourself hooked up with a strange group, did you not?"

He laughs.

He is a lovely young man. Too lovely for his own good.

I fear that his anxiety disorder may recur.

Does he have more cave paintings in him? More artistic salvation?

We finish our wine in silence.

With his goodbye, he hugs me the way I imagine a son would hug his mother. I would like a different kind of hug, but beggars cannot be choosy.

Sometimes my ears are full of night.

In bed, I think fleetingly of Tevis; mostly, I think of my Lucas.

I do not know how long I had been asleep when I was awakened by the intrusion of hideous howling. It seemed human, but, if so, a human in great pain or despair. I rose, threw on my robe, and headed outside with a flashlight.

Soon I found the source of the howling: Perry Ellis.

He was stationed under the large water oak by the pond, swinging his corn knife wildly. He must have sharpened it, for he was slicing into the bark of the oak with ease.

"Have you lost your mind?" I hollered at him. "Go on ta home!"

He paused to look up into the night sky as if he thought he had heard the voice of God. Then he began wailing quite pathetically, and something in the tenor of his cries angered me further.

"Get off my property! Do you hear me? Go on ta home!"

I stomped off.

I returned to my cabin.

I heard nothing further except the groaning and moaning of my heart.

July 24

The day has passed. I sit at my fire pit. Marauder is at my feet to comfort me. I do not know where Jacob is.

What occurred this morning was horrible.

Horrible.

I cannot even think about it without trembling.

It all began quite early, soon after first light, when, as I was wetting a towel to drape onto my neck—my accustomed practice before I strike out on a walk on these warm mornings—I heard Marauder barking and, in the distance, Jacob braying. The sound of the mule appeared to originate near the pond.

A sick feeling gripped my stomach.

I began to walk hurriedly in that direction.

Gracious goodness—what I found!

Jacob, innocent accomplice, was stomping his feet restlessly nearby; his eyes were wild and preternaturally alert.

Perry Ellis, naked, the new rope around his neck, dangled, twisting slowly, one bare foot brushing the ground. He was choking and gurgling.

Then I began to run. I yelled words, but I do not now recall what they were. I was so unsettled that intense lights throbbed in my vision, making it very difficult to see what needed to be seen.

A suicide attempt.

The demons had won over Perry Ellis.

The new rope had been tossed over the limb of the water oak. It was holding tight, and yet what obviously had occurred is that the boy had misjudged the length of rope when Jacob had been exhorted to run from under his rider.

In pain, the rope burning and digging into his neck, threatening to strangle him, Perry Ellis spun as helplessly as ever a body could. At first, I was literally paralyzed to act because I could not keep from staring at the boy's manhood. Then something prompted me—I do not know what—to snatch up the corn knife and slice at the taut rope.

It snapped instantly. Perry Ellis crumpled to the ground.

He groaned and writhed as I knelt by him. I held his face in my hands and said, "Oh, oh, oh."

For a run of terrible seconds, my mind was absolutely blank.

Fortunately, something resembling good sense took over, and I ran to get my Lucas, not knowing that the worst was yet to come. It took a few minutes to rouse him and get him out of his trailer. As it happened, within another five to ten minutes, Tevis showed up on his bicycle. I stood back as my Lucas and Tevis ministered to Perry Ellis. They gradually helped him to a sitting position.

But his face boiled with rage.

I cannot recall specifically what then transpired except that as my Lucas was talking with the angry, distraught boy, there was a flurry of movement. Suddenly, Perry Ellis was on his knees, the corn knife in his hand. He swung it at my Lucas and Tevis several times, growling and grunting maniacally as he did. He scrambled away from them, and then the image that sticks in my mental filter is one of blood.

So much blood.

Blood that seemed so bright. So alive.

Then a cry of pain that must have been heard on the dark side of the moon.

Perry Ellis, with two chops of his razor-sharp corn knife, had removed most of three fingers and the tip of another on his left hand.

Shock in his eyes, Tevis turned my way. "Give us that towel!" he exclaimed. "Hurry!"

I complied.

Then I sank to my knees.

And I sobbed dry, body-wracking sobs.

I watched as my Lucas and Tevis rushed Perry Ellis, his

hand wrapped in my wet towel to staunch the blood, away like men on a battlefield in the midst of combat assisting a fallen comrade.

I continue to sit alone. Tevis came by to look in on me. I was surprised to learn that after loading Perry Ellis in the pickup, my Lucas insisted that they take the boy to Sister Speakes.

"She managed to stop the bleeding," Tevis explained. "I guess maybe he'll be all right." He sounded doubtful.

"I want to blame it on demons," I said. "But what hurts is that it is not the whole truth."

As if a curious entropy had set in, and there were simply no words to be said, Tevis patted my hand and kissed my forehead and left. I did not see my Lucas until the next day.

Jacob lingered close to the cabin.

His black, gem-like eyes sought me out once.

His look appeared to ask for forgiveness from one who was unforgiveable.

July 25

My guilt is bottomless.

Perry Ellis: his attempted suicide and his mutilation of self are my fault.

Perry Ellis—why could I not have mothered him into a birthing of the one he might have become?

Have I been feeding off all the madness surrounding me?

Am I simply cruel and heartless?

By late morning I am seeking solace in Emerson, searching for his remarks on the self's sovereignty over matters of life and death. In his *Journals*, I locate the passage I need again to read:

"As soon as your friend has become to you an object of thought, has revealed to you with great prominence a new nature, & has become a measure whereof you are fully possessed to gauge & test more, as his character become solid & sweet wisdom it is already a sign to you that his office to you is closing; expect thenceforward the hour in which he shall be withdrawn from your sight."

Emerson thought grief was shallow. Each day is an end in itself. He survived personal tragedies—deaths. At least in my case, Perry Ellis was not "withdrawn from" my sight. Not permanently.

Early afternoon, my Lucas and Tevis wade through the heat to tell me that, indeed, Perry Ellis will live, sans a part of him, and that he is resting at his grandmother's. I question that he was not taken to the Sweet River Hospital, but my Lucas claims that Sister Speakes is trusted by every black person within miles for medical emergencies. Perhaps he is right.

When they leave, I continue, selfishly, to feel sorry for myself. The unexpected arrival of Cavatina interrupts my blue voyage. She asks about Perry Ellis. I relay all that I know and, quite suddenly, she bursts into tears. As I attempt to console her, she pulls away and begins, savagely, to stab at her stomach and legs with the cross and dagger that Perry Ellis carved for her a few weeks ago.

Screaming at her, I wrestle her to the floor and somehow manage to dislodge the weapon from her hand before she does any serious harm to herself. For a long run of minutes, I hold her, I rock her, and I talk softly to her, words coming from some daimōn of autonomous imagination I never knew existed.

The mother I was not destined to be.

She calms herself.

I am shaking to the soles of my feet, and yet I am glad that Cavatina feels something. *Something.* Nearly an hour later, I let her go to meet Jenny who apparently was waiting for her.

I sit at my table and stare into the shadows of oblivion.

I must struggle to keep despair from taking over my cabin.

I fear that if I do not get a hold of myself I shall be forced to murmur a farewell to my sanity as I mentally cross the river of good mind.

Invisible minutes pass.

Whitman lives in my barren womb—from him, however, I keep hearing the gestation of things to be left behind:

"Let me glide noiselessly forth;
With the keys of softness unlock the locks—with a whisper,
Set ope the door O soul."

But, unlike, Whitman, I am not certain what I shall find within.

July 26

Iwake to discover a rain-dark snail inching across my kitchen floor.

A good omen, I believe, but when I venture out to greet the dawn I see that Resurrection Fern has been splashed and smeared with blood. Cavatina's blood? The blood of Perry Ellis? I cannot be sure. I am dismayed and seek shelter within the shell of my existence.

I spend most of the day cleaning my cabin. It feels good to do so. It prevents me from thinking too deeply.

With nightfall, my Lucas arrives, Allegra in tow. Joy surges through me at the sight of him, and yet he does not look well. His eyes are wet; he embraces me, and I return the embrace and tell him that I love him and always will. He thanks me.

The three of us sit at my table, its surface still bearing a hatchet scar. Allegra is shocking to see: the skin on her cheeks and forehead is flaying. She continues to be ghostly pale and emaciated, her form barely more than skeletal. She is walking death. She exudes a faint stench that rudely tickles my nostrils.

"I need help," says my Lucas.

We talk about things; we talk as if Allegra is not there. As I listen, I realize that the incident involving Perry Ellis has served as a sobering catalyst for my Lucas. He has been breathing despair and hopelessness.

"It's no use," he says. He looks from me to Allegra, and I understand. "Nothing can ever be the same as it was."

I press my hand upon his. We sit, the two of us, as icons of grief—Allegra is a stone work of Thanatos. And there is a moment in the deepening silence where everything suddenly changes. Here is what happens: Allegra begins grunting, a sub-human sound that is shattering to experience.

"Stop!" my Lucas exclaims. "Damn you to hell, stop!"

But she does not or cannot.

And then he slaps her, a hard slap that turns her head. It has the dead thud of a hand striking the carcass of a slaugh-tered animal. Allegra slumps slightly to one side. The grunting ceases.

My Lucas, tears bubbling, looks at me with a desperation I can hardly bear.

There is a pleading from every fiber of his body: "God, I can't stand this! I can't go on with this!"

I rise and hold his head against my stomach.

Oddly enough, I feel calm and certain.

"What you must do," I say, "is merciful."

I can tell that he is distraught and yet listening.

"This is not life—for either of you," I say.

Then he whispers, "I need a sign."

At that moment, I know how I can help.

"When you are ready," I say, "come here alone, and we shall talk with our father. He will know what to do."

My Lucas is relieved.

Gently aiding the corpse that is his companion, he trundles his way back to his trailer.

I stand and stare into the woods. I think of poetry I have read, but the precise poet and the poem escape me.

Darkness the darkness that was already my darkness.

I hear something winging among the tall pines—darkness filled with a feathery whistling.

In bed, I think of my Lucas and the violent necessity build-ing in my thoughts.

I sink from dark to deeper dark, from dark to rest but not a final resting place.

Mine is a torn world well worth forgetting.

July 27

I am awake at 4:00 a.m.

People crowd my consciousness: Cavatina, for example—I feel sorry for her. I do not know how to help her, and I do not know why I have such a deep-seated longing for a daughter. Too late. Too late for that. I think about Perry Ellis. Oh, I am tossed by guilt, and yet I am also angry at him for what I perceive to be extreme foolishness.

Mostly, I think of my Lucas: I shall help him. I know a way to help him.

Allegra: unfortunately, there is only one way she can be helped.

Then I tense.

Marauder and Jacob have been put to voice by something or someone. I sit up in bed. Quite suddenly, I hear a tremendous thrashing, a movement in the woods that sounds more than anything else like an elephant rambling through the thicket.

Gracious goodness!

Something passes in a thundering and a horrid grunting.

Could the bowels of the haunted ground beneath the woods have generated such a noise?

Two hours later I am still awake. I rise to find a perfect pearl of a full moon in the west. Marauder and Jacob have calmed some, but they are uneasy. As dawn edges nearer, I fix coffee. I have just taken a sip when I hear a man's voice approaching. I go to my door where I see a flashlight larger than a car's beam. And I see a hulk of a man.

It is Mr. Bonnard.

He is toting a rifle that appears to dwarf even those owned by my Lucas.

Mr. Bonnard is huffing and puffing. When he speaks, his tone alarms me.

"Miss DeGresse, you should oughtta get back in your cabin and close and lock your door, ma'am—there's danger for sure out here."

I invite him in. He is reluctant at first.

"Have you been giving chase?" I say.

"Yes, ma'am, and what … the thing is …"

But he does not finish his sentence. He plops down at my table, unshoulders that massive rifle, and wipes his mouth. I can barely believe my eyes to see him, this giant of a man, trembling. He mops his face with a red handkerchief; he removes his cap and rubs hard at his scalp.

"The thing is," he continues, "God in heaven, I've done seen somethin' like uh monster out there. Never seen nothin' like it before—nothin' like it atall."

I pour him coffee, and I give him time to get a hold of himself.

But I am astonished to see this: Mr. T-Bone Bonnard is frightened.

Very frightened.

So in good time, he tells me what he has seen.

The Beast.

No, not something imaginary. This apparently is real.

"A wild boar," he says, a tremor in his voice, "and I'd swear on the Bible this creature is twelve feet long or better and more than uh thousand pounds—I ain't lyin'."

I assure him that I do not assume he is.

"I did not know wild boars could reach such a size," I say.

He grows very quiet. He turns in his chair and stares towards the door.

"This one did." He pauses. "I saw … I saw this gentleman's tusks, you know, up close when it done surprised me, and I swear they's most near a yard long. Like nothin' you've never seen." He hesitates. Sighs deeply. "I got two shots off at 'im. He done ran on through here 'hind your brother's trailer."

"Yes," I say, "I believe I heard him."

Several times he emphasizes that I should be careful with such an animal prowling about. We visit a few minutes longer; he is impatient to be gone. Then I mention that my mother is coming to live with me, possibly soon. His demeanor transforms instantly. He asks that I alert him when I have learned which day she will arrive. I tell him I shall.

He shoulders the rifle, thanks me for the coffee, and lets first light usher him into the woods like some mystical guide.

For unknown reasons, the existence of the giant, wild boar does not terrify me.

Why would such a creature waste his time on a thin and lonely woman?

A brief, late afternoon shower beats upon the roof of my cabin. I venture forth in the steamy aftermath accompanied by Marauder who stays at my heels rather than lead the way. Such a brave dog!

I go to Cat Bells.

Someone is within, for I see a faint light.

When I crawl inside, I find Tevis sitting akimbo in front of his wall painting. He seems glad yet subdued that I have come. Sky is back at their tent by the pond.

"He's failing," says Tevis.

"I am sorry to hear that," I say, and I mean it.

I mention Mr. Bonnard and the wild boar. Tevis believes he heard it, too.

"I feel that bad things are coming," he says. "I feel it."

I sense that perhaps he is right.

Then I find that he has scooted closer to me and that there is something he needs to say or confess. I pat his hand; I have no words. He looks into my eyes and says, "I'm taking Sky to Sister Speakes. She's the last hope. The last one."

I do not try to dissuade him, for in his voice I hear something I understand implicitly: this is what he must do, and he must do it.

I slip away from him; he needs space and time.

Night is the beast that surrounds.

Naked, I stand in candlelight in front of my long mirror, and I pledge to myself that I shall take back my Lucas from the Nightmare-Life-in-Death creature that holds him in thrall.

Naked, I step out of my cabin, lift my hands, and draw down the moon.

I feel it in my sex.

From the center of the darkness within me, my life calls out again and again.

I close my eyes.

And when I open them, I see, out beyond Resurrection Fern, a small girl—not real—her face as black as the night.

Almost there.

A Child of Always.

July 28

Seems as if everyone near me is dead but refuses to die.

The night and much of the morning pass without any sign of the wild boar. When I take my Lucas a batch of biscuits, it is evident that he knows of the creature. He warns me, much as Mr. Bonnard had, to be wary wise regarding it. But he does not believe it will approach human habitation unless food has become scarce.

My Lucas says that he will come to my cabin tomorrow.

He needs to hear our father's vision of the future.

We embrace solemnly.

Back in my kitchen, I turn to find Tevis at my door.

"It's Perry Ellis," he says. "I think you should call someone."

"Why? What has happened?"

"He's up by the pond, and he's … he says he's looking for his fingers."

"Goodness, no," I murmur.

Does no one take responsibility for the boy's actions? He has no business being away from his home so soon after his injuries.

As we walk briskly towards the pond, Tevis says, "I told him they're gone—his fingers. Some animal probably got them."

I see Perry Ellis down on all fours. He is sniffing around for what is lost forever. His hand is heavily bandaged. A salve of some kind glistens on the rope burn on his neck.

I shall have my Lucas contact the boy's family. Or perhaps not. What could they do?

I cannot watch this.

I turn, but Tevis stops me. He points beyond Perry Ellis.

And there is Cavatina. She is helping with the search.

Off away from both of them is Jenny. She is weeping softly.

"Let them all be. Just let them be," I say to Tevis.

Late evening, I sit at my fire pit and lose myself in a reverie with the flames. Tevis shows up. Somehow I sensed he would. Sadness weighs him down. He sits and talks as if he is confessing something to himself.

I am not there.

"Sister Speakes claims she can't help Sky," he says. "His death is rising."

And I recall the night of my swamp walk with Allegra: *This is the track of death rising.*

"I am terribly sorry," I say, ashamed that I have nothing more to offer.

"I know you mean that," he says. "Thank you."

When he has left, I block out everything. Read nothing.

I begin preparing myself to call forth a ghost and to save the man I love.

July 29

During the day, I set out the bottle tree. I want the company of good spirits only.

I have not heard the wild boar return. At dawn, I woke to the sound of Perry Ellis howling at the setting moon as he searched for what no longer belonged to him. He did not stay in pursuit for many minutes. Perhaps he is beginning to accept his loss. Or his madness.

I should warn him about the giant boar; but then again, the boy would not be apprehensive about imminent danger—his life does not mean enough to him for that.

In my kitchen, I think about poisons. I do not want Allegra to experience pain, if, indeed, she is capable of experiencing pain. But poison seems impractical—what kind could dispatch someone no longer alive?

I wait.

I suddenly envision another possibility.

The day is a long, hot summer's worth of seconds.

I am sitting by my fire pit when my Lucas arrives.

He is alone.

He wears an unsettled expression; his eyes twitch. He embraces me. He sits down and holds my hand and says, "Jessica Love, what if she doesn't realize she's dead?"

So I am thus aware of what he has been thinking about.

"What do you mean?" I say to force him to clarify.

"I mean … if I tell her, if I explain … maybe she will die peacefully. She'll be released—on her own. She will accept how she is. She will go ahead and die and not just be dead."

His expression is powered by hope.

I let him dangle. What else could I have done?

I cannot lose him. I cannot.

"Let us go inside and hear what our father advises."

My cabin is lighted only by candles as we sit at my table and begin the séance.

Am I evil?

No, I am a woman in love who must do what is necessary. I am less than nothing without my Lucas.

May the gods forgive me.

Across the table we hold hands. I close my eyes. I pretend to fall into a trance. This theater of deception unfolds so smoothly that I am quite surprised. I almost subscribe to the fiction of it all.

Why does my Lucas believe this nonsense?

I am glad that he does.

At just the right moment, I squeeze his hand and maintain that I have made contact with our father. He knows the dilemma my Lucas faces. He has an answer.

My Lucas trembles.

I set my jaw in order to continue with the hoax.

"He says for you to go to the cave. Take Allegra to the abyss. He says you will be forgiven. All shall be forgiven."

It is as simple and horrid as that.

My Lucas offers a weak smile and thanks me.

"Our father is right—I know he is," he says.

And it is finished.

When my Lucas says goodnight and clambers away, I hear him singing a lovely, dark, dark lyric of redemption and salvation.

I hate myself, and yet I am relieved.

July 30

Ninety-nine degrees today.

A record high for east Alabama.

My woods bake and rise like homemade bread.

Throughout the day, I wonder whether my Lucas has done the deed—I feel, wickedly, a bit like Lady Macbeth, but there is no damned spot of blood on my hand. I suppose I am a bit like her husband, but I see no daggers of the mind—no ghosts, in fact, and the trees surrounding my cabin do not march against me.

Around noon, Cavatina slogs in from the heat. She has been crying again. She asks what can be done about Perry Ellis. I tell her that he will give up his fruitless search in time.

"You need to move on with your life," I say.

But in this wild, young, and often vile woman I notice a change—as if she is carrying a new self within.

I ask her again how she feels about Allegra. Does she accept that her sister cannot go on as she is?

"When that bastard raped and buried her," she responds, "maybe she really died, you know, and hasn't been alive since."

I sound like an echo chamber.

"She cannot go on like she is. It would be cruel."

I sense that Cavatina agrees. I sense that she will accept matters quite easily when Allegra is gone.

"What are you going to do now?" I say.

She shrugs and wipes her nose.

"Shit, I don't know. Who the fuck cares?"

"I care." Then I hesitate. Words flow over which I seem to have no control. "Jenny cares. I think Perry Ellis still cares."

"I'm done with him. He's gone out of his head. I can't do nothin' for him—doncha see that?"

"Yes, I do." And I reach for her, and I hold her. "I shall try to be here for you."

She pulls away, nods, and smiles a sickly, hopeless smile.

Then she leaves like a phantom passing into nothingness.

Sunset is serene and achingly peaceful.

I sip at a glass of iced tea near the flameless fire pit. I talk gibberish at Marauder and Jacob. I listen to the birds of gathering twilight.

I feel good despite myself.

In fact, I lapse into something like a daze just before Tevis strides into my presence. His face is a mask of alarm. He borders upon being in shock. I rather expected that he might become aware of the leprous ritual.

"Miss DeGresse, oh, my God. I saw your brother and Allegra go into the cave, and so I followed and …"

I reach out for his wrists.

I smile.

"Yes," I say, "I know. It seemed the best way, though it must look horrible beyond words to you. She is gone forever. She has fallen through to the end of night. And now my Lucas has another chance to live."

He is shaking his head, not in disbelief but rather, it appears, in deep sadness or regret.

"I'm afraid, Miss DeGresse, you don't understand."

But when he explains, my entire body rejects his words. I am angered. I shout at him that I do not believe him. I do not believe him for the simple reason that my Lucas promised he would never leave me.

He gave me his word.

Days later, when I replayed the moment, I vaguely remembered screaming at the top of my lungs before shattering like a crystalline figurine.

July 31

The entries for July 31 and August 1 were recorded late on the evening of August 2 when I was finally physically and spiritually capable of doing so. Gentle Reader, please bear with me, for what remains in my memory of those days amounts to fuzzy spots of time and space.

Never had I so wished to die.

Never had I become so determined to live.

On July 31, I seem to recall that Tevis helped me search for my Lucas: in his trailer, the woods and, especially, in Cat Bells. My Lucas and Allegra had vanished—Orpheus with his Eurydice.

I do not know how I would have gotten through the day without Tevis who not only tended to me but also to his deathly ill friend, Sky, in their tent by the pond.

At one point, I seem to recall Tevis asking whether authorities should be contacted. He alluded to matters such as insurance and other barbed and twisted issues that connect us to the real world.

At another point, I believe he asked me whether he should try to retrieve the bodies. To which I believe I replied, "Why? *Neither* is dead. The girl who cannot die and the man who cannot live."

The temperature hovered around one hundred degrees by mid-afternoon.

August 1

I did not celebrate the arrival of the new month.

I could not.

A strange, summer wind blew all day or so it seemed, a wind inhabited by an admonitory presence, a wooing voice whispering of loss, death and grief.

Jenny and Cavatina and Tevis ministered to me.

I do not recall eating or sleeping. But I must have.

I stayed in bed as if a helpless invalid.

What kept me sane?

Well, what has always kept me sane: books, poetry, and language that touches the soul.

While Jenny and Cavatina nursed me, Tevis talked to me and read to me.

Some of it has stuck with me. For example, his recounting of Thoreau's grief in response to the death of his brother and, more so, his choosing to read Whitman's "Each Has His Grief" which includes the following velvet defiance:

So, welcome death! Whene'er the time
That the dread summons must be met,
I'll yield without one pang of fear,
Or sigh, or vain regret.

But, of course, Tevis knew that I needed most of all to hear my dear Miss Emily Dickinson: "I measure every Grief I meet/ With narrow, probing, eyes—/I wonder if It weighs like Mine—/ Or has an Easier size."

And my favorite: "Grief is a Mouse—"

A mouse that keeps running up the clock and from corner to corner of my cabin before nesting in my heart.

August 2

Jenny and Cavatina give me a sponge bath. I am beyond
embarrassment. They help me dress and fix my face and hair.
What woman does not feel better when she is presentable?

On the edge of tears, I thank them.

Later in the morning, I am greeted by the beatific smile
of Tevis, and I sense, painfully, that his days on my property
are numbered just as the mortality of his friend, Sky, is closing
down.

He informs me that Perry Ellis has, again, been looking for
his fingers.

"It's a sad, sad sight," he says. "But I shouldn't bring up sadness. I'm sorry."

"Sadness and sorrow flow in our lives the same as hope and
gladness," I respond.

He has my volume of Dickinson and claims that he has found
a special poem for me: "The Soul has Bandaged moments"—a
perfect choice, as I see it. I cannot repress a chuckle. We sit at my
kitchen table. He reads in his lovely, lovely voice tinged with a
feminine air.

"The Soul has Bandaged moments—
When too appalled to stir—
She feels some ghastly Fright come up
And stop to look at her—"

Yes, indeed, some "ghastly Fright" has stopped to look at
me, to see what I am made of, I assume. And, thanks to Jenny,
Cavatina, and Tevis, my spirit experiences "retaken moments."

I shall live.

When Tevis leaves, I imagine that I hear my Lucas singing. It is a sign, of course, that I cannot let go. I cannot. Grief opens up strange worlds, of that, once again, I am reminded.

And that most curious, warm wind blows up again. What does it presage?

In this case, rain: a steady, heavy at times, shower late afternoon. And there is something I cannot resist. I walk out into the cleansing, cooling moisture. I tilt my head back and open my mouth, and I drink. I stand. I shiver. And I am baptized by Nature. Born again? Or is it, more precisely, a case of being birthed for the first time?

Evening finds me in bed surrounded by candles.

I am drifting upon a silent sea of solitude when I become aware of an intruder.

At first, I am frightened witless. But then I see that it is Perry Ellis. He steps to the foot of my bed, teary-eyed, his mouth working, no words escaping.

I smile. I clear my throat.

"Gracious goodness, Perry Ellis, your visit is a surprise. Do you want me to make coffee?"

He shakes his head. He tries once again, unsuccessfully, to speak.

And so I seize the moment. I feel a choking, then a release, a flushing of my body and my spirit. I murmur in a raspy voice,

"Please forgive me."

In his dark, twitching eyes, I think I see that he does.

Then he is gone.

I sleep a dreamless sleep of meager self-reverence.

August 3

The bottle tree has been smashed.

By the Beast? By the wild boar? Perry Ellis?

It does not matter. I must, on my own, keep evil spirits away. But I reprimand Resurrection Fern for not being a better scarecrow.

I sit outside. I wish it had rained more so than it did, for my woods remain dry and, I fear, prone to fire.

I know who my visitor will be even before he enters stage left.

It is Tevis.

"I brought you something," he says, handing me a pencil portrait of himself. "Hope it doesn't seem egotistical that it's of me. I thought you might, you know, want it to remember me by."

I cannot speak. I see him through the prism of my tears.

He has come to say goodbye.

We sit quietly, speechlessly, for several minutes before I can find voice. I take his hand in mine. I look into the young man's eyes, eyes much too beautiful for my world or any other.

"If angels truly exist," I say, "then you are one. You have been wings of light in my dark life."

He gently guides my head to his shoulder.

"I'll never forget you, Miss DeGresse—Jessica."

I disappear into thought: of how alike, in some ways, we are—losing what we love most—he, Sky; me, my Lucas. And questions I want to ask, but choose not to: Where will you go? Will you return one day? Will you love again?

Odd it is, but when he left me, it seemed that he was merely an apparition.

Or a fleeting ray of sunlight.

My Tevis: I grew to love him, not sexually, not woman to man, but human to human, spirit to spirit.

And loving, I have learned, is our most difficult task, our most impossible burden.

.

August 4

Yes, I am alive again.
Resurrection Jessie.
All this day, Whitman's astonishingly beautiful poem, "Night on the Prairies," rings in my ears, with its devastatingly appropriate final line:

I see that I am to wait for what will be exhibited by death.

August 5

The wild boar thundered close to my cabin in the night scattering Marauder and Jacob and leaving one casualty in the wake: Resurrection Fern. Her cross beams were broken as if they had been matchsticks.

I found tracks: ugly, cloven-hoofed stabbings of the earth.

Passing through as he hunted the creature, Mr. Bonnard stopped long enough to repair my scarecrow. I put her head in place and cloaked her in black.

Edgy and impatient, Mr. Bonnard, out of politeness, stayed for coffee. Sweating profusely, he gulped down my brew. In a weakened moment, I told him that my Lucas and Allegra had gone away. His piggy eyes squinted at me: I am a poor liar. He did not, however, challenge my unconvincing narrative.

Thanking me for the coffee, he rose from his chair.

"I got to bring down that monster—I got to. It's done got in my blood, doncha see?"

I said that, yes, I could see that. I cautioned him to be careful.

He smiled faintly.

"Y'all do the same, ma'am."

Later in the day, another scorcher, the hummingbird flicked in for a visit.

When I saw that tiny, lovely bird, I knew that I had to go to Cat Bells.

August 6

Cavatina, who showed up after still another fight with Jenny, joined me in a pilgrimage of sorts. Under the spell of twilight, with flashlight in hand, we trekked up to Cat Bells.

"Do you understand why I must do this?" I said.

Cavatina shrugged.

"Doesn't matter. You got your reasons—nothin' else matters."

Perhaps she was right.

Again I intuited that she had become a slightly different person.

Somehow more completely a woman.

It took more courage than I realized it would to crawl through the opening. I almost sounded retreat. I might have, in fact, had Cavatina not been there to urge me on. We paused at the wall painting—the masterpiece of Tevis. Her mouth opened in a vapid form of awe, Cavatina looked from the dancing figures to me.

"You miss 'im, don't you? Tevis, I mean. You really liked that guy."

Quite suddenly, I choked up.

"I did. I truly did."

"Maybe, you know, he'll come on back some day."

I shook my head.

"Best for him if he does not. He has his whole life …"

A separation of speech and thought took hold.

Cavatina picked up the exchange.

"I never knew much of nothin' about 'im, you know. Where's he's from. His folks. Whether he had brothers and sisters and shit like that. I just knew nothin'."

In a whisper, I said, "Me, either. It is as if he were truly an angel. As if such beings truly exist."

"You think that's maybe true?"

It was my turn to shrug as all agnostics must shrug.

"Hold my hand," I said as I gently pulled her towards the abyss off to the right.

I sensed where they had been. I imagined that I could smell the ghost of my Lucas, his scent. Why oh why did he plunge into the darkness with her? Why?

"Fuck, this is scary," Cavatina murmured.

We held each other. I angled the beam down into the seemingly bottomless opening. I wanted to hear singing. I wanted to.

But only the deepest, more profound silence rushed up to taunt my sadness.

August 7

I am sitting by the pond stroking Marauder's head and ears. Jacob noses away the surface scum to drink his fill.

I am watching Perry Ellis.

In the early morning light, turtles are seeking a good spot for sunning. Perhaps that is what I am doing: basking in my unwillingness to believe that my Lucas is gone. Has perished. He said that he would never leave me—why should I doubt that now?

Digging, scratching, sniffing, Perry Ellis resembles a dog, more dog even than Marauder. My thoughts smack of racism, I assume, but like most Southerners, I believe I know the difference between authentic racism and a sound and sane appraisal of another person.

"Perry Ellis, please give up this senseless activity," I say.

Of course, he does not.

And I feel a need for confession. It hits me the way hot flashes apparently seize older women experiencing their change in life.

"I did not want to see you mutilate yourself." As the words float into the stillness of the day, I think suddenly about Cavatina and the night she arrived bleeding from the mindless cutting practiced by her and her bloodthirsty group of young idiots.

Perry Ellis is pulling up tuffs of sedge grass and peering into the dirt left behind.

I shift to what is truly on my mind.

"Will you please tell me why my Lucas disappeared into the darkness? Did your God or Jesus make him do that? Did your demons? Perry Ellis, are you listening?"

Obviously, he is not.

I dab at my forehead and cheeks with my wet towel.

I feel a twinge of madness behind my eyes.

"It appears, my friend," I say, "that you need some help."

And so I am soon on all fours at the side of Perry Ellis. He does not seem surprised that I have joined in his search. At first, I feel as ridiculous as a goose, but then as I claw at the ground with my fingers, something causes my body to shiver with excitement and my heart to drum with joy.

What I am seeking is seeking me.

August 8

I receive unwanted news.

My mother will be moving in with me tomorrow.

I spend much of the day rearranging my cabin to accommodate her: I shall be sleeping on the cot; mother will have my bed. I am tempted, of course, to put her in the trailer once shared by my Lucas and Allegra, but I am not able to bring myself to violate that residence. I see it now as a shrine of sorts, at least until my Lucas returns, with or, hopefully, without Allegra.

I know that must sound crazy.

So be it.

Towards evening, I am exhausted. I sit by my fire pit and drink a glass of wine. I toast myself Whitmanesquely. Call me selfish, if you will. I do not care. I drink a second glass of wine, and, certainly, it may be that I become a tad bit tipsy, for I have forgotten to eat today. Night and stars swirl, and I feel that I am being watched by the mystical Child of Always somewhere in the ineffable.

"Miss DeGresse, ma'am?"

A man's voice drives the imaginary child away.

On legs atremble, I rise to greet Mr. Bonnard who, as usual these days, is toting his mammoth rifle, one large enough to bring down small dinosaurs, or so it appears to me.

He sits and shares a glass of wine with me.

He senses, I believe, that I am on the cusp of becoming inebriated, but his comportment is polite. He tells me that he is confident he will be successful in hunting down the monstrous wild boar.

And one thing more.

"Miss DeGresse," he says, "that ole swamp witch, Sister Speakes, she's dead. Done passed on. I found her stiff as uh cedar knee in her shack yesterday."

"Whatever did she die from?"

"It 'pears to me, ma'am, she done had all the life scar't outta her."

We sober a few moments in that news, and then I inform him that my mother shall be taking up residence with me tomorrow. He receives my words with much gladness. But he does not allow himself to linger there.

His face, by degrees, reflects a dark seriousness. He rises and then stalks off purposely into the woods in search of his primordial prey.

Left alone, I retrieve one of my volumes of Whitman, and I read aloud the opening stanza of a poem that fits my mood like a glove:

"As I ebb'd with the ocean of life,
As I wended the shores I know,
As I walk'd where the ripples continually wash you Paumanok,
Where they rustle up hoarse and sibilant,
Where the fierce old mother endlessly cries for her castaways,
I musing late in the autumn clay, gazing off southward,
Held by this electric self out of the pride of which I utter poems,
Was seiz'd by the spirit that trails in the lines underfoot,
The rim, the sediment that stands for all the water and all the land of the globe."

Castaway that I am, I wonder whether the fierce old mother Whitman alludes to is endlessly crying for me.

I can only shrug and take this electric self to bed.

And fear tomorrow.

August 9

My mother does not appear wilted by the heat.

It is mid-morning; she has arrived, wearing a dress and a wide-brimmed hat to fend off the sun. Beneath the hat, her hair has been combed, and I am surprised to find that when I greet her outside my cabin, she says, "Hello, daughter."

We embrace. And I momentarily crumple. I do, oddly enough, feel like a daughter again.

"It is good to have you, mother."

Why, I wonder, have I been dreading her coming?

Her worldly possessions have been condensed into two suitcases and a large purse. She smiles, not nervously, but rather as if relieved.

Helping her is the Haitian housekeeper, Marie, a dumpy, dark-complexioned woman in her fifties, I would guess. She seems put out. She strikes me as unpleasant, but perhaps the incessant heat is to blame. Wearing a shapeless, white dress and something like a turban, also white, she glares at the surroundings; apparently, she does not like the woods. She smells bad, and her face is pocked and scarred. A male friend her age named "Robert" is with her. He is tall and very thin with shifty eyes, and yet a charming smile. He wears a purple fedora. His skin is even blacker than Marie's, but I do not believe he is Haitian. Are he and Marie lovers? I do not know.

But what steals my attention completely is a little girl: timidly, she is hiding behind Marie. Her name is "Liane," and she is perhaps six or seven with hair so black that it shines, trained in tight, plaited rows rounding back to pig tails that resemble strands of barbed wire. She is wearing a blisteringly white dress, frilly and simply darling as if she is about to attend an Easter service. She has on patent leather, black shoes, the kind we once referred to as "church shoes." She is related to Marie.

Her face—gracious goodness—possesses flawless skin, quite black, an open expression, radiant smile, though judiciously offered, and brilliantly white teeth. But what arrests me are her eyes.

For I have imagined those eyes most of the summer.

Fireflies flicker there—visionless or seeing more than can be seen.

Candle flames within bottomless pools.

Marie calls her "Li-Li."

I keep thinking that I know her.

My Child of Always.

I edge closer to her. She is a beaming presence, and yet darkness lurks there, too. A snatch of poetry comes to mind: "deathwards progressing/To no death was the visage."

Oh, dear, what is this?

I lean down to say hello to her. At first, she is shy, but then she collects herself and reaches up to pat my cheeks. I am dizzied by the rush of sheer strangeness I feel—fear and bliss at once. She does not merely touch my body; she seems, as well, to touch my spirit.

I stand up on legs that threaten to give way.

I turn to attend to my mother.

Marie and Robert, I am told, have located a place to live in Sweet River; they will take Li-Li with them. The news disappoints me; I am sorry to learn that the girl will not be staying. I almost beg them to let her reside with us, at least for a few days.

One bit of weirdness before we part company: Li-Li slips away from the cabin. When we find her, she is on her knees, head bowed, hands folded in prayer. She has placed herself at the foot of Resurrection Fern.

I experience a *frisson*.

Late afternoon, Mr. Bonnard makes his appearance. He brings flowers—yellow roses—and an assortment of fresh fruits and vegetables as well as bottles of wine. I smile in noticing that he

wears no cap, shoulders no rifle, has on a clean shirt and overalls, and has slicked back his hair with some kind of perfumed
oil.

My mother recognizes him. In fact, she seems pleased to see
him.

I drift out away from the cabin to allow them to sit in the
kitchen and visit.

August 10

The first night passes uneventfully.

My mother and I are having coffee and toast with grape jelly. We chat in mother/daughter tones. I find little or no madness or senility in her.

"Do you remember this cabin?" I say.

"Oh, yes. Dalton loved it."

"I do hope you will like living here. My life is plain and simple. But I am content," I say, sounding rather like a bad imitation of Thoreau.

My mother seems comfortable. Alert. At ease. At home. I wish that I were not so surprised or perhaps even disappointed at how sane and healthy she is.

And then she poses a question that generates an odd twinge in me.

"Mr. Bonnard isn't married, is he?"

I tell her what I know of him, which is not much. It hurts me that she does not ask about my Lucas. But then, what could I say in response?

I am showing mother my ferns when Marie and Robert come up the main path. Robert carries two small suitcases, and I see that Li-Li is trailing them, skipping and singing snatches of something I cannot decipher.

Striding up to us, Marie says, "She wants be here. Li-Li. She belong here."

And with that, the little girl rushes forward to hug my mother and then to hug me. I am inwardly elated.

The understanding is that they will return for her in the weeks ahead.

I am thinking immediately that I shall fix a place for Li-Li to sleep on the floor next to my hearth.

Then Marie takes me aside. Before she can speak, I say, "She is such a precious little girl. I shall take good care of her."

Marie shakes her head. With an edge of intensity in her voice, she says, "She can find your darkness. You can't see."

"I do not understand you," I say.

"Here is deep matters," she follows, adding an unreadable smile.

I do not like the woman.

I want to protect Li-Li.

Mother her.

Was Marie trying to say that Li-Li could shine with a mystic light that was not always heavenly? Then so be it. I would not be a stranger to a mystic light.

That evening, I discover that Li-Li loves candles as much as I do.

We surround her makeshift bed with them; she smiles like glory.

The three of us sit up and talk about nothing at all. Li-Li speaks almost no English and just a few inelegant pieces of French, I believe it is, and some ill-sounding dialect. However, my mother is excellent at asking her yes/no questions that she understands, and thus there is communication.

Before we turn in, Li-Li and I step out and say goodnight to Resurrection Fern.

My Child of Always seems in awe of her.

August 11

Mr. Bonnard returns.

Li-Li and I go outside while he and my mother sit at my table and talk. I hear muted laughter. It is quite obvious that Mr. Bonnard is in love with my mother. I do not know how I feel about that.

I decide to take Li-Li to the pond. She is wearing shorts and a halter top. She goes barefoot, for that is what she prefers. On our way, she sings some little ditty in a language from nowhere, I would guess.

Marauder and Jacob are curious of her. It is almost as if she is another animal, not one they fear, but one unknown to them. And strange it is that she can not only embrace their undivided consciousness, but she also can mimic, with startling accuracy, the bark of Marauder and the bray of Jacob.

At the pond we find Perry Ellis in his fruitless search.

"I have a visitor I want you to meet," I say to him.

But it becomes evident that when he senses her presence, he is frightened.

He even growls at her.

"Perry Ellis! Gracious! What is wrong with you? This is a precious little child—how dare you act this way!"

When I have finished snapping at him, Li-Li steps forward and takes him by his bandaged hand. She caresses it. She whispers words over it.

Perry Ellis seems stunned.

Minutes later, when he slinks away, I notice that there are tears in his eyes.

August 12

Over coffee, my mother surprised me once again.

"How is Lucas? Has he gone away?"

I hesitate. It is a threshold moment, and I am unsure how to cross into it.

"Well, yes, in fact, he has. But I am hoping that he will return soon."

My mother smiles to herself.

"Did he … has he found love in his life?"

Throat suddenly burning, I glance away.

"I believe he found love, yes, but love is such a difficult thing—it is so hard to be a keeper of love."

My words sound foolish, trite. She nods as if to rescue me.

"He once sang so lovely," she says. "Has he continued to sing? Did that awful war take that from him?"

How should I respond?

I am astonished at how clear and articulate she is.

"I believe he will sing again," are the words that escape from me.

My mother seems pleased.

And a bit later, Mr. Bonnard appears at my door asking whether he might drive my mother over to see his tavern. I smile at his nervousness. They shuffle off like a perfectly matched couple.

I fix breakfast for Li-Li. She loves oranges and melon.

We go exploring in the woods with Marauder and Jacob as bodyguards.

Early afternoon, we take a nap. Then, later, Cavatina drops by, and, as I expected, she is instantly fascinated by Li-Li. The

three of us head for the pond. I am relieved to find that Perry
Ellis is not there.

We sit and watch turtles.

Li-Li is drawn to the tattoo on Cavatina's throat.

"Doncha never get one of these," she says to the girl. "I'm
tired of havin' it. Wish I could get the hell rid of it, but it's like a
real mess to do that."

Her curiosity pricked, Li-Li smilingly approaches the tattoo.
She whispers something neither Cavatina nor I can hear, then
she places her left hand gently onto the snake's head and rubs it.

"Watch it, little girla, that ole bastard might bite," Cavatina
jokes.

Li-Li, delighted, claps her hands and skips away.

Cavatina gazes at me.

"She's a trip, ain't she?"

I nod.

"She is remarkable."

We stroll into the woods and wind around again to the
cabin.

And I notice something as the three of us sit at my table and
drink iced tea.

My breath catches.

I find a hand mirror and give it to Cavatina. I can feel the
sudden heat of the fear that is generated in her.

"Oh, this is too fucking weird," she exclaims, her eyes fixed
upon the tattoo, or, rather, where the tattoo had been.

When Li-Li steals off to be in the presence of Resurrection
Fern, Cavatina, and I examine more closely the area in question.

The tattoo has, indeed, vanished.

In a hollow tone, Cavatina murmurs, "Does she know voo-
doo—you know, magic shit, zombie shit? How the fuck did she
do this?"

"I have no idea," I say.

And that is the truth.

In the company of Li-Li, I was made increasingly aware that my
property was surrounded by other worlds: invisible, miracu-
lous, wondrous—terrifying. Around Li-Li, my inner most self

floated freely, beyond my control.

She caused me to think of Hawthorne's *The Scarlet Letter* and, naturally, of Hester's daughter, Pearl. I located a passage in that great book, a description one could easily apply to Li-Li:

"Pearl's aspect was imbued with a spell of infinite variety: in this one child there were many children, comprehending the full scope between the wild-flower prettiness of a peasant-baby, and the pomp, in little, of an infant princess. Throughout all, however, there was a trait of passion, a certain depth of hue, which she never lost; and if, in any of her changes, she had grown fainter or paler, she would have ceased to be herself;—it would have been no longer Pearl!"

Yes, Li-Li could have been Pearl's dark sister.

Child of Always. Child of Infinite Variety.

I wait up for my mother to return.

She assures me that she has had a wonderful day.

She and I must have a talk soon.

I kiss Li-Li goodnight. She purrs like a large housecat. She possesses an animalistic warmth.

As always, I go to sleep listening for the song of my Lucas. My Orpheus.

August 13

While Li-Li plays with Marauder and Jacob, my mother and I muse over our coffee. I guide her carefully to the issue at hand. She is firm and lucid and sensible.

"Tobias and I need one another."

"But you hardly know him."

"That's not true. There's a history you aren't aware of."

So I listen as she judiciously narrates a long ago, apparently not-so-innocent attraction the two of them had for each other. When she finishes, she says, "Do you think poorly of your mother now?"

"Oh, no," I say. "I am pleased for what has happened."

That falls short of the truth. On the other hand, I am startled by how much my mother has changed from the last time we spoke months ago. Will she experience a relapse into her personal darkness?

I change the subject to Li-Li.

I ask my mother whether she has witnessed the girl's strangeness.

"She is from a land where she would not be so different from others. Yes, I have seen that she has been marked. But she would not, I am sure, harm either one of us."

I admit to moments during the day in which I sense that the ghost of our father lurks. But I assure myself that it is only my imagination. In contrast, the powers of Li-Li seem most certainly real.

An afternoon shower breaks the heat somewhat.

At twilight, I make an unsettling discovery.

Li-Li has collected small animal skulls and bones and has piled them into an altar at the feet of Resurrection Fern. When I find her praying and chanting, I stop her and pull her back into the cabin.

I love this child.

Can I ask her to cease being herself?

No, if I did, I fear that she would vanish.

August 14

There is rain this morning, light and timid, without passion. I decide not to interfere with any of Li-Li's ritualistic tendencies. Her world is a mystery to me as is, I believe, mine to her.

Very early this morning she gave me quite a shock. Before dawn, I stirred; when I glanced at her sleeping area, she was gone. My heart clawing in my throat, I grabbed my flashlight and headed outside. I did not wake mother.

Though I checked near Resurrection Fern first, I sensed that the child might have been drawn to the swamp, and so I tracked off in that direction, Marauder at my heels.

"Why did you not protect our little child?" I said to him, but received no answer. On the path to the swamp, I smelled the wild boar—my fear roared; it sickened me. I found myself thinking about the death of Sister Speakes. Nahollo Swamp was, indeed, a realm in which one could be frightened to death or, at the least, have the life siphoned out of one.

I thought of Allegra.

Then I pushed on.

Until I found her.

In a trance, it seemed, she stood staring into a black wall of wild vegetation. What captured her attention, what seduced her soul, I do not know. I grabbed her up and took her home. She did not protest until we reached the cabin where some mysterious state took her over: she suddenly hissed, drawing and expelling her breath through her teeth, changing her face, indrawing it so that it became skull-like.

I was so unsettled that I wept.

And that broke the spell.

Gently, tentatively, Li-Li's fingers caressed my face.

By afternoon, the rain had completely disappeared. While mother napped, Li-Li and I ventured to Cat Bells. Along the way, I thought about Li-Li's trek into the swamp. I thought of how Thoreau had taught me to see Nature as a force, a process, an energy—Li-Li allowed me to see and sense even more: that within Nature exists a supra-sensible realm that she could enter and I could not.

Only a Child of Always could.

It was not surprising that Li-Li was entranced by the cave, given its darkly mothering presence. We stopped, of course, in front of the painting, the magnificent work of Tevis. Li-Li brushed her eyes over it as if she were able to read its secret language: perhaps she could. I told her all about Tevis, how wonderful it was to have him as a friend; I talked as well of my Lucas.

I led Li-Li to the abyss.

I should not have, yes, I know.

It was a moment out of space and time. In fact, I do not remember it now with any precision except for this: on the lip of that endless darkness Li-Li leaned out and began to sing one of her haunting, quietly surreal lyrics. And then she stood back from the edge and—I confess that my eyes could have deceived me—she raised her arms to her side, and in the spray of my flashlight, she rose an inch or more from the floor of the cave.

Gracious goodness, she levitated.

Or so it seemed to me.

Frightened, I quickly took her hand and led her back outside.

But as we exited, I could swear that I heard a faint, ineffable singing as it rose up from the abyss like smoke from Nature's central fire.

August 15

I welcome the chill of Deep Kill Creek.

So does mother, I believe. I do not, however, know what Li-Li welcomes, what darkness she invites into or rejects from her existence.

It is shortly after lunch, and the incredible heat of the summer of 2010 is building. My brain has been dulled, but I manage to think about the dream mother shared with me this morning at breakfast—one centered on "Alice," the child who died, my sister, Alice Amelia DeGresse. Mother dreamed that the ghost of Alice appeared to her as a grown woman to grant her permission to do something she has been struggling with.

"An odd dream," I said.

"Alice glided up to my bed, and she didn't even have to speak. I knew. I knew she had come as a sign that life moves on. Love can grow in unexpected places."

I sensed, of course, what she was alluding to.

But guilt seethed within me. I wanted no ghosts in my life.

What I think I wanted was to confess.

And so here I am, wading out towards the only deeper hole remaining in the shrinking waters of the creek. I hear Li-Li splashing and laughing just like a normal little girl. Mother is laughing, too, for she has removed her shoes and is having trouble with the slippery bottom as she wades behind me.

I decide that it is time.

I shall not recall my exact words—they are not important—and yet my need to purge myself of guilt goes beyond language. I start in.

"Mother, you must, in fairness, know what I have done and what I contributed to."

She smiles and brushes an unruly strand of hair from her forehead. She is listening, and I open my heart and there in the inexorable, purling stream I tell her what happened the day her husband passed away. I tell her what I did. How I believe I was responsible. Then I shift to the days following the birth of Alice. I tell her what I did. I talk of my orchestration of her—my mother's—mental breakdown. I confess to my jealousy of Alice. I tell her that I was probably a factor leading to her death.

I did horrible things.

And I have been punished: eros has not been willing to enter my life.

Mother's smile does not fade. She reaches for me, but suddenly I cannot accept her mercy or her forgiveness, and so I plunge forward into the deeper water. And I stumble and fall.

And the world bubbles and gurgles and my head roars beyond sound.

I thrash.

And I feel the death that has been growing within me blossom.

Then a strong hand on my arm.

Mother pulling me to the surface.

Mother embracing me, embracing her child.

Later, back at the cabin, I sit in warm, dry clothes as mother fixes me a cup of coffee and Li-Li skips around outside, singing a song to Resurrection Fern. My mother does not need to tell me that she forgives me—I feel it in her presence.

I muse to myself: so this is what it is like to be saved by the one person I did not want in my life.

How strange. How passing strange life is.

Thoreau knew.

Nightfall.

Mr. Bonnard has stopped by. He is more determined than ever to kill the wild boar.

His mystic Beast.

But not mine.

August 16

The inevitable exchange humbles me.

Over our morning coffee, mother talks some more of her feelings for Tobias Bonnard, her "Toby." She talks of companionship in terms that strike me almost as metaphysical. I have never had the kind of companionship she alludes to.

Never.

I am jealous.

"Toby has asked that I come and stay with him. I have said that I warmly desire to. But I would like your blessing."

"Everything about this," I say, "is inappropriate."

I am wrong, of course, and I know it.

Deflecting my position, mother says, "I will take Li-Li if you like. But it might could be that you would enjoy keeping her here with you. The companionship, I mean."

I nod.

I hate myself for not being happy for the woman who brought me into this world.

"I do want Li-Li," I say.

August 17

L i-Li speaks in a voice as soft as the turning of a page.
The voice of endlessness.

She and I walk, nosing out every corner of my property. Nature is so vast and unknowable that, at times, I find myself in a land other than the one on my owner's deed. It is an Edenic realm, and yet, of course, there must be serpents in Eden—real ones, such as the large timber rattlers we come upon occasionally. They are venom dealers. They coil and thrum in their savage grayness. Marauder, shedding good sense as he grows older, barks foolishly close to them.

Li-Li is even less afraid of them.

I have to stop her from pursuing them and handling them.

She likes for me to lift her on to the back of Jacob; together, they exist as one in an ever-moving center.

At the pond, we see the passing shadow of Perry Ellis, cheater of death. I can see that he wants to be friends with Li-Li, or, at least, to lose his fear of her.

Returning to the cabin, we escape the heat. Cavatina and Jenny join us for lunch. The two of them seem to have patched up their differences for the time being. We eat melon and strawberries and cream. I notice that Cavatina's tattoo is still absent. She glows. She is becoming a woman. Growing up. Ripening. She, in her unkempt way, is beautiful, and Jenny drinks in that beauty with nearly every heartbeat.

Evening frames a portrait of the two of us only: Li-Li on my lap, the fire pit aflame. I feel joy. I feel free, for the most part, from guilt. It is the best moment of the entire summer.

I hold Li-Li and hum in her ear.

I scan the approach of darkness and wonder whether the Beast is out there. I doubt it, but the giant, wild boar is, for I continue to hear its distant thunder as it crashes from the swamp and along the boundaries of my property.

At night, alone with Li-Li, I come closer than ever before to the wildness of my essential, innermost self, and it is there that I converse with a community of eternal realties.

My eyes shut, I can imagine the voice of my Lucas, a ghostly aria rising.

When darkness falls heavily, Li-Li and I say goodnight to Marauder and Jacob.

Our final task is to say goodnight to Resurrection Fern.

She has, I believe, a certain intelligence in her artificial eyes.

But then, even a scarecrow can be wise beyond its straw.

August 18

This morning, when Li-Li chased after Marauder who, in turn, was hunting some wild varmint, I strolled along until I met my ghostly double. She stared at me like a concerned friend and said, "When will you stop being content?"

I shivered hard. I was troubled, but I brushed the encounter aside.

Her words haunt me.

I have started to imagine that I am imagining things.

At the pond, I am pleased with a sudden development: Li-Li and Perry Ellis are sitting together under a willow tree. They are too far away for me to hear what they are talking about or even if they *are* talking. I sense an ineffable symbiosis between them. I hope it lasts.

The turtles. I perceive the mystery of the universe as I study them: they are sunning on logs and rocks in the pond. They have mastered the inscrutable possibilities of doing nothing. They remind me that there is a holiness in *seeing*, and who I am determines *what* I see.

Late afternoon, my mother and Mr. Bonnard visit us. They continue to be happy together.

Eros found.

A journey ended in the meeting of lovers.

She, terrifyingly alone; he, terrifyingly lonely.

Both seduced by mutual assertions of humanity.

After we bid them goodnight, Li-Li and I sit out as has become our habit. I place starter sticks and dry grass in the fire pit, and then it is that I am witness to still another of Li-Li's wild talents.

With the blazing stare of her eyes, she ignites the fire.

August 19

The horror of this day will be a long time dying.

Li-Li has fallen asleep as the stars appear. She is, I believe, understandably exhausted. But thoughts of death keep me wide awake. My mind swirls in a muddy eddy. I reach for the poetry of Dickinson to help siphon off the strange images of mortality that unsettle me.

"Death sets a thing significant
The eye had hurried by,
Except a perished creature
Entreat us tenderly."

Perished creature echoes weirdly among the auditory hallucinations I am experiencing. I read a few lines more of Dickinson:

"It was not death, for I stood up,
And all the dead lie down.
It was not night, for all the bells
Put out their tongues for noon."

Tragedy struck this afternoon as Li-Li and I returned from Deep Kill Creek. I seem to recall hearing a bark and an eagerly meaningless growl from Marauder. Then I heard his ear-piercing yelp.

I saw the timber rattler glide away.

I saw blood on Marauder's shoulder.

I hollered like a swamper. I grabbed up the bitten dog and pressed him to my bosom and ran back to the cabin, Li-Li following. Because he appeared to be shivering, I covered him with a heavy towel. He groaned. His throat swelled up as if he had swallowed an orange.

I held Li-Li and rocked her and whispered to her to allay her anxieties.

I had no medication for the dying animal. I was helpless, and I was in that state until my mother and Mr. Bonnard happened to stop in as twilight approached. Mr. Bonnard escorted us out of the cabin. He stayed inside with Marauder. I do not know what he did or how he ministered to my dog in pain.

Not many minutes later, he announced the death of Marauder.

We did not move the unfortunate dog.

We covered his body completely with the towel.

I cried. My mother attempted to comfort me. She offered to stay the night, but I told her that I would be fine.

She and Mr. Bonnard left reluctantly.

I thought about where I should bury Marauder.

Li-Li commiserated with me in her quiet way. She helped me light more than a dozen candles. She hugged my neck. Then I sat alone at my table; I put my head down on it and sought oblivion.

I came back to reality when, through the thick silence of my candlelit kitchen, I heard Li-Li speaking in a language known only to the gods. Hunkered over the body of Marauder, she chanted, patting at the dog's shoulder, her own body jerking slightly as if possessed.

I believe now that she was.

I heard her hiss, distinctly, like a snake.

And then she collapsed to one side, and I stumbled down to her.

And Marauder suddenly, miraculously, raised his head and whimpered.

Gracious goodness.

I do not understand what occurred.

Li-Li continues to sleep.

Having drunk quite a lot of water, Marauder is lying near my feet, his breathing irregular, but he is alive, and I do not know how he possibly can be.

I listen to the night.

The wild boar is roaming.

I close my eyes and shudder.

I have witnessed the transmutation of the material of death into the substance of life.

August 20

More violence today.

Around noon, we received approximately one-half inch of rain. While I was thankful for it, as usual this summer brief showers have not brought much relief from the heat. After the rain, I felt very tired. Marauder literally and figuratively dogged my heels; I do not think that he quite accepted that he was alive. He did not wish, it seems, to leave the cabin.

I prodded Li-Li into going down with me for a nap, but when I woke fifteen to twenty minutes later, she had left her sleeping area. I went outside and called for her. And then a terrible sense of foreboding poured through me like ice water.

I found her a hundred yards or so south of the cabin. I came upon her as she stood staring at the massive boar as it munched on fallen acorns. I could not fully believe the size of the creature. Seeing it made my arms go limp. Li-Li was not more than sixty to eighty feet from the beast; she appeared to be eating the image of it with her eyes—it was a gaze of worship, or nearly so. I was glad that she did not protest when I quietly tugged her safely away.

No more than an hour later, Mr. Bonnard and two other men shambled up to the cabin. The men accompanying Mr. Bonnard—I do not recall their names—were lean and hungry and scruffy characters who were either pulpwooders or scavengers, stitching out a living in the swamp. Like Mr. Bonnard, they carried large rifles and a glint in their eyes that spoke of killing and things primitive.

Of course, I told Mr. Bonnard of our sighting of the boar. But his attention was drawn to something else: to Marauder. It was obvious that he was dumbfounded. I maintained that it was simply one of those cases of a creature only seemingly being dead. I did not share what appeared to be the truth of the matter. However, I sensed that Mr. Bonnard was not comfortable around Li-Li—no, he did not express his feelings, and yet that discomfort inhabited his eyes.

The hunters headed off in the direction I pointed to.

Li-Li and I ate peaches and played with Marauder.

Within an hour of Mr. Bonnard and his cohorts having left the cabin, the stillness of the afternoon heat broke quite suddenly. There were loud, ugly reports—a dozen, maybe more. I could smell smoke from the guns. Li-Li's eyes grew large and sad. I held her. For a few seconds, she did not appear to be breathing.

I am weary this evening. My heart beats irregularly.

Li-Li is asleep, or, at least, I believe she is.

Earlier, Mr. Bonnard returned to tell me that the boar would no longer be a threat to us. After dispatching the creature, he and his men went back to his tavern before coming back with a camera and with shovels. They buried the boar right where they killed it.

"Thank you, Mr. Bonnard, for this service," I said. "Yes, we shall sleep less fitfully knowing this animal is not on the prowl."

"You're welcome, ma'am. It was uh giant," he said. "Like uh freak uh some kind. A swamp monster." He shook his head, and then he leaned over and petted Marauder and seemed to study him. He glanced at Li-Li—I do not know what he was thinking. "Ma'am, your mother, she's doin' good 'n fine." He paused. I heard his throat rattle wetly. "She's uh blessin' in my life, uh God's honest blessin'."

I nodded.

And wished that I could have been happier for him.

August 21

Now I believe I know what Li-Li is capable of.

At first light, I found that she had left the cabin. I had a very good idea where she had gone, and so when I reached the area in which the massive boar had been buried, I gathered her up and took her back with me.

The empty grave yawned, a raw wound in the earth.

It was well into the morning before the inevitable occurred: Mr. Bonnard returning to the scene of the kill as if to assure himself that he had not dreamed up the destruction of such a huge animal.

His hands were shaking, his face pale and sweaty when he entered my cabin. I poured him a glass of iced tea. At first, he was speechless. I fetched him a cold rag for his face.

"Ma'am, d'you happen to notice anybody out wheres you saw the boar yesterday?"

"No," I said. "What has happened?"

In truth, of course, I honestly did not know.

Like a man in a trance, he said, "Somethin' dug up that boar. It's done all the way gone outta that hole we put it in."

"Perhaps coyotes did it," I suggested.

He shook his head soberly.

"No, ma'am. No way. 'Cuse me, but there's no way in hell coyotes or no other animal in these here woods did what's been done."

I said nothing more.

Mr. Bonnard left, a man on the brink of losing touch with reality.

Late afternoon, Li-Li and I tended to Resurrection Fern. We dressed her anew, Li-Li attaching small animal bones to her and staining her clothing with the purple juice of beauty berries that grow so plentifully near the cabin. Our efforts generated a hideous result: Fern resembled a corpse ready to stride off into the everywhere.

But Li-Li was not finished.

I could not stop her.

She suddenly bit her arm savagely, then dabbed her fingers in her own blood and smeared it on Fern's face before whirling several times and flinging herself prostrate at the feet of the scarecrow.

The blood on Li-Li's arm reminded me of my first meeting with Cavatina.

The summer of 2010 had come full circle.

I thought of the resurrected boar—Li-Li's doings.

Mostly, I thought of my Lucas.

Of how much I needed him.

And of sensing who had the power to return him to me.

August 22

The darkness of Cat Bells is cool and velvety.

My flashlight sprays across the work of Tevis, those stick-like figures dancing in fear and bliss—dancing their artist out of his anxiety. I miss Tevis. I miss the part of myself that pulsed in my blood when he was near.

Li-Li brushes her fingers over the surface of the wall. She gurgles something, words perhaps, but I do not understand what she is trying to express. I wonder what marvelous things she sees in the art of Tevis.

I wonder whether she understands why I have brought her back once again to this cave.

I take her hand, but she knows the way.

On the edge of the abyss, we squat down. Li-Li searches my face; I am trying not to cry.

"I want my Lucas," I mutter. Tears scorch my cheeks.

Expressionless, Li-Li turns from me back to the endless darkness at her feet. She raises her arms. She moves her hands as if she is about to take flight. And once again, I see—or imagine—that her feet leave the cave floor a few inches.

I feel the extreme heat radiating from her body.

I whisper, "My Lucas, please come back."

And then she sings, my Li-Li.

For a matter of minutes, I would guess, she sings like some mythical bird or beast and her voice echoes in a heartbreakingly lovely fashion, filling my ears, filling my spirit. I lose track of time. I sense, in fact, that I am no longer in my body.

Here is what shatters the spell.

A voice from below.

I want, oh, I want so much to stay and hear more.

But Li-Li takes my hand and leads me out of the cave, out of a wilderness of darkness and yet hope.

For what remains is the waiting.

August 23

Before dawn, the full moon rides low in the west.
I sit out with Li-Li by the fire pit. Marauder and Jacob are near. Resurrection Fern is not far away.

I have fixed myself a cup of coffee. I have poured a glass of warm milk for Li-Li.

My Lucas has returned.

I know it. Somehow I know it.

And I do not attempt to stop her when Li-Li steals away like a ghost. Her destination? I think I know that, too.

And so I wait.

Until a ghostly voice seeps through the night.

I turn, and Li-Li is holding the hand of my Lucas.

The darkness of the cave has temporarily blinded him.

I stand to greet him.

He does not smile. He cannot smile.

Allegra is not with him. Cannot be with him, I assume.

"Oh, my sweetheart," I exclaim.

Almost alive, he raises his arms and the chill of his embrace swims in my blood and numbs my heart.

August 24

He slept near Li-Li, my Lucas.

They share a symbiosis I cannot begin to understand.

In the sobering light of day, my joy at the return of my Lucas begins to evaporate, for he barely exists, a nightmare-in-life much as Allegra existed and, quite possibly, continues to exist deep in the bowels of Cat Bells.

But I shall cling to the shadows of my gladness.

I take the cold, clammy hand of my Lucas, and I say, "You kept your promise. You did not leave me. You came back. And you will always, always, always have a home here on this property. You will always have my love."

I tell him about Li-Li, her magic, but I am not certain that he comprehends a word I say. I ramble on about the return of our mother, about how she and Mr. Bonnard have found each other, and I touch upon the death of the wild boar and its resurrection. I even mention Perry Ellis and Cavatina, although I cannot now recall what I told him.

For it does not matter.

Late morning, I busy myself baking for my Lucas—he must be starved; of course, I fear that he is not. I fear that the sensate enjoyments of life for him have dissolved. I shall pretend that they have not.

The oblivion brought on by domestic chores is broken when I feel the ground beneath me quake.

"Heavenly days," I murmur.

I do not even bother to remove my apron because I realize suddenly that Li-Li and my Lucas are off somewhere together.

The quake is followed by an explosion—I envision flames even before I see them.

Standing together some thirty yards or so from the trailer, Li-Li and my Lucas are holding hands. In joint reverie they watch the conflagration, and I know that Li-Li started the fire. Perhaps my Lucas urged her to.

I want to call out for them to extinguish the blaze, but that would be pointless. The fire is somehow good. Right. Necessary. Life is growing and burning, and for my Lucas, burning his abode completes something.

That night, my Lucas and Li-Li and I sit out by the fire pit and quietly enjoy each other's company. As a pleasant surprise, Perry Ellis joins us. My Lucas embraces him robotically, and yet I imagine a touch of warmth is exchanged.

I look around at them, the full moon showering down on our gathering, and I say, "I love each of you, for you are sometimes darkness, but you are my community, bringing light to shine upon my loneliness."

I try not to be disappointed when I gesture for Li-Li to come inside for bed and my Lucas chooses to drift off towards the swamp, Perry Ellis with him like his shadow. I hear them "whoop" like mystic beasts.

They are disembodied spirits now, and they will haunt the night.

August 25

Another revelation of wonder and magic today.
A smiling Perry Ellis at my cabin door. When I ask him where my Lucas is, he merely shrugs. I invite him in for coffee. Li-Li goes to him and hugs him. My home space is filled with smiles. I am suspicious.

Putting his hand to his throat, Perry Ellis says, in a raspy voice, "Miss Jessica."

I have to smile at that, the first time he has called me by that name.

"Whatever are you up to, Perry Ellis? Have you swallowed the canary?" I glance at Li-Li; her smile tells me nothing.

"Dis be a miracle," he says. He looks down at Li-Li. "Dis child of good demons, she did it."

"Goodness," I say, "you are the very voice of mystery."

Then he raises his left hand which he had kept hidden beneath my table.

I blink at it, obtusely regarding the significance of his gesture.

He wiggles his fingers.

"Dis be a miracle," he says again.

I gasp.

The fingers he had violently removed weeks ago had somehow returned. Grown back. In the flesh and moving again.

When evening arrives, Perry Ellis and my Lucas are nowhere to be found. The swamp, I assume, has claimed them. And so Li-Li and I kneel at the foot of Resurrection Fern, our goddess. I pretend to be filled with worship, but I am faking it. Li-Li is not.

We sit near our evening fire.

I think of my Lucas, of Perry Ellis, of Marauder and of the wild boar. I gaze at Li-Li, and I am bereft.

She terrifies me.

And I love her and need her. She is my missing piece.

August 26

Cavatina is alone when she knocks on my door this morning. She has something on her mind—it is almost comical to see this lovely young girl/woman attempting to be serious.

She accepts my offer of iced tea.

Li-Li crawls into my lap. Cavatina smiles at her wistfully, or so it seems to me.

"How you been?" she asks me.

I open up with the news of the return of my Lucas and the miracle of Perry Ellis and his fingers.

"My Li-Li is responsible. Perry Ellis calls her a 'child of good demons,' and I believe he is correct."

Cavatina, perhaps accustomed to all the strangeness of the summer and the magic of Li-Li, does not seem in the least astounded by my news. She stalls for the better part of a minute before she says,

"I've got a shitter of a problem."

I laugh softly.

"Elegantly put."

"I'm serious."

"I can see that."

She shakes her head as if in defeat. I wait for her to speak again.

"I'm so fucked," she mutters.

"How so?"

By now I have guessed. Again, I let her hesitate.

With a deep sigh, she says, "I got myself pregnant ... and ... it's so stupid, so fuckin' stupid."

I rub the back of her wrist as she cries real tears. Li-Li and

I console her as best we can. A question comes to my lips. I should not ask it, but I do.

"Is Perry Ellis the father?"

She does not respond, and I am glad.

In May, she—part girl, part woman—will give birth.

August 27

We are out early, my Li-Li and I. My thoughts center on Cavatina as I wade across a trickle of Deep Kill Creek. I hold Li-Li's hand. I feel sorry for Cavatina, as her life seems a damned-up stream.

Minutes later, Li-Li and I are sitting on a sand bar. The girl is intensely quiet. She knows something. And, suddenly, I think I know it, too.

"You will be leaving—is that what you cannot say?"

Pressing her face against my shoulder, she moans and groans.

I feel how much I need to mother.

I feel how much I have missed out on in my life.

And yet Li-Li has too much wilderness in her for me to tame. She is the child of Thoreau's darkest imagination.

"You are a wondrous darling," I whisper to her.

Just before supper, a thunderstorm cracks open upon the roof of the cabin, and the pouring rain rocks us like two children in a cradle.

In bed, my heart breaks into a hundred pieces.

I listen.

I hear my Lucas singing hopelessly in the distance like a caged animal.

August 28

My Lucas exists in the nowhere, never, not.
In the terror of Nahollo Swamp. In the blackness of Cat Bells.

He exists, but he cannot live.

Morning ushers in visitors.

Perry Ellis, smiling shyly, brings Li-Li a beautiful, dark wood carving about the size of a sand dollar—depicted on the flat disk is her face, smiling the power of secrets. He and Li-Li embrace, and I choke back tears.

Not long after Perry Ellis steals away, my mother arrives. She firms up what I already know: that Marie will be coming for Li-Li.

"I don't want you to live alone, dear," she says.

I smile self-deprecatingly.

"I am not fit to live with another, though I would like to be."

She stays until Marie and Robert approach the cabin. Li-Li clings to me, hooks her arms around my waist. I hate what I realize I must do. I ask everyone to leave Li-Li and me alone. What I want is to run off with her into the swamp and live like the wildest of creatures. But I cannot do that.

We embrace, wordlessly, for ten minutes or more.

During those moments, I rehearse a cruel release.

I pry the girl from my body, and I lean down and attempt to generate firmness in my voice. I must try to be convincing.

"You are not wanted here," I exclaim. Her eyes begin to fill. I shove her towards the door of the cabin. "Go on away from here—take your darkness with you."

She looks at me, pleadingly, for the better part of an eternity.

"You are *not* wanted!" I shriek.

I turn and go to my bedroom.

I hear her wail.

I hear Marie talking with her softly. My mother packs up Li-Li's things.

I cannot bear to see that beautiful child one more time.

I would die of sadness.

That evening I sit with Marauder and Jacob at the fire pit.

I have never, never felt so alone in my life.

My Lucas and Perry Ellis are off chasing after phantoms of themselves. Resurrection Fern senses a great loss.

And I … I shiver in lonelitude.

This much I know.

I need to be the keeper of someone who has departed.

August 29

The light morning rain is dreary, Poe-like.

I walk into my woods hoping to meet the ghost of Thoreau.

Instead, I come upon Perry Ellis. He is petting the wild boar, a much-bloodied creature covered in blotches of red clay from being unearthed. On a sturdy limb of a tall, sweetgum towering over the scene of boy and boar, is my Lucas; he is cooing like a turtle dove.

It is a primitively peaceful scene.

Yet terrifying and surreal.

Not one that I can belong to.

All afternoon, I read Dickinson, drawn especially to those poems in which she alludes to summer.

"Further in Summer than the Birds—
Pathetic from the Grass—
A minor Nation celebrates
Its unobtrusive Mass."
Two lines in particular punch at me with their resonance:
"As imperceptibly as Grief
The Summer lapsed away—"
Oh, and that has been so true, I think to myself.
"Our Summer made her light escape
Into the Beautiful—"

And I want so much to "escape" into that beautiful essence

that autumn sometimes brings—and yet, is that possible given my givens?

I read until tears blur the words:

"'Twas here my summer paused
What ripeness after then
To other scene or other soul
My sentence had begun."

I dry my tears.
I miss Li-Li more than any poet could put into words.

August 30

I cry again at dawn, naked, in my bed.

Unclothed, I use a footstool to help me climb upon the back of Jacob and grasp his mane. Marauder follows as we walk to the pond, Jacob so muscular, so powerful between my legs.

I no longer care for propriety or civility or decency.

I think about Li-Li's inexplicable magic. Is it possible that I only imagined it? Perhaps I am, after all, an unreliable narrator, sister to those unreliable narrators in the tales of Poe. But, no, I tell myself, others witnessed Li-Li's wild talents.

Astride Jacob, I watch my turtles sun themselves.

In that looking, I begin to feel ashamed.

Gracious goodness, what is wrong with me?

My senses fully returned, I sit in my cabin and mop my face with a cool rag.

Is there nothing left for me?

At twilight, my fire pit flaming like an oracle, I received an answer from the outside, from the unexpected.

Cavatina joined me, her manner timid. She literally approached as if she carried the world on her shoulders. We embraced. We sat, and I watched as her bottom lip quivered— she could not speak.

I told her that Li-Li had been taken away.

I told her how much I had grown to care about that child.

"I had to say mean things to her to get her to leave," I said.

Cavatina nodded.

She was trembling.

She appeared old.

She looked up at the stars, and she pressed her fingertips onto her stomach. Then her eyes met mine.

"Would you take my kid? Would you—you know—take care of it and love it, boy or girl?"

I half could not believe my ears.

Silence surrounded us like a thick fog.

"Are you certain of this?" I said.

She nodded vigorously.

"No fuckin' way I could be a good mother. Not ready for that."

I reached for her.

I reached for both of them.

August 31

Call it one more touch of evil.

Call me wretched. Call me vile.

But I slept well after Cavatina left.

This morning I talked with Mr. Bonnard who is in the area carrying his obscene rifle. He is hunting the wild boar again. He believes he is hunting a ghost.

Early afternoon, I am not surprised to find Jenny at my door. She has braved the horrible heat for good reason. I invite her in, but we cannot be friends, and we do not understand precisely how it is we have become enemies.

"Do you know," she asks, "the meaning of the name 'Cavatina'?"

I admit that I do not.

"I looked it up," she says. Her face contorts, a despairing hopefulness tracks across it. "It means a short song of simple character. Cavatina. It's a lovely name."

I agree.

"She is capable of making difficult decisions," I say to get out in front of what I know is coming.

"Please!" she exclaims in a harsh whisper. "Oh, please! That child. That child is what Cavatina and I need to be couple, to be a family—to live in a strong, loving way. Surely you see what's best here."

"I do."

"Then … then you agree that she's making a mistake. You'll tell her so, won't you? You'll explain that you just can't take the child—it would not be what's best here. You'll tell her?"

Her face judders miserably.

I wait until she knows what I must say. I wait until her torture appears to anneal her.

I clear my throat.

"No," I say, "I shall do no such thing."

My final act of darkness?

Perhaps.

I shall be derided for my selfishness. So be it.

And yet, I would not, *would not* otherwise diminish myself.

Would you, Gentle Reader?

Beyond Summer

One day, the girl who would not die met the man who could not live.

That is where this narrative truly began. And so I wait for a new life, a new narrative: September, October, into the sudden chill of November.

My paths have led nowhere the dead wish to go.

I crave community over solitude: my companions are the people of the grave. More so, they remain the people of the word: Emerson, Thoreau, Poe, Hawthorne, Melville, Whitman, and Dickinson—whatever would I have done without them?

Frosty November evenings, I sit close to the fire pit and read to Perry Ellis and my Lucas. One night I read from Emerson's wise poem, "Blight."

I adore the following passage:

"Our eyes
Are armed, but we are strangers to the stars,
And strangers to the mystic beast and bird,
And strangers to the plant and to the mine."

The "mystic beast?"

It is ourselves, and we shall always be strangers to the mystic spirit within us.

Marie and Robert went north, and so I must assume that I shall never see Li-Li again.

But I live and shall hope for an authentic death one day, to be at peace with mortality. In the meantime, I wait for Cavatina's child. It will be a girl, I know it. Do not ask me how I know. I shall name her "Lovelia"—"Love" for short—and she will be a Child of Always, a shadow of Li-Li, that wondrous, little magical soul.

Here I am.

Alone with my darkness. Unforgiven in my heart. Making no petition for a life beyond this one, living until I end my song.

I light a single candle.

Perhaps the world is not yet lost.

But I am tired.

Love, let us rest in this.

About the Author

Stephen Gresham has been publishing commercial fiction since 1982. His books include:

Moon Lake
Rockabye Baby
Half Moon Down
Dew Claws
The Shadow Man
Midnight Boy
Abracadabra
Runaway
Night Touch
Blood Wings
Demon's Eye
The Living Dark
Primal Instinct (Written as "John Newland")
Just Pretend (Written as "J.V. Lewton")
Called to Darkness (Written as "J.V. Lewton")
Night Shapes
Haunted Ground
In the Blood
The Fraternity
Dark Magic
The Book of Moonlight
Crossing the River of Good Mind
Deadrise

Visit www.stephengresham.com for more details about Stephen's publications and writing career. Stephen also enjoys hearing from readers at greshsl@auburn.edu.

Curious about other Crossroad Press books?
Stop by our site:
http://store.crossroadpress.com
We offer quality writing
in digital, audio, and print formats.